BEDTIME STORIES FOR ADULTS

Suffering, Sweat, and another!

Brenda Turner

Suffering

Diana was aimlessly waltzing around the watchtower, looking for something interesting to do as she passed by the other participants who were having fun with each other.

"It must be fun to hang out with somebody and do things you like," she reasoned to herself.

It's not because she didn't have the chance to hang out; she did go on a couple of coffee dates with Clark, which she didn't genuinely enjoy, mostly because he doesn't recognize her preferred drink, which is iced mocha.

She played video games with Wally, which disappointed her, Shayera and John are too preoccupied with each other, and Martian Manhunter is as hard to talk to as a brick.

She arrived at her quarters and sat on her bunk. Diana's face was painted with a big pout as she sat in her bed, bored and irritated. An idea flashed through her mind as her lips curled into a mischievous grin.

She went to the monitor womb when a man can be seen typing something on a dimly lit keyboard. She can see from the torch and the flickering lighting that this is, without a doubt, The Dark Knight himself.

She moved cautiously towards her, hoping to catch him off guard and making him jump, but sadly...
"Don't you have something more important to do, Princess?" Before she might even make a pass, he whispered sternly.
Diana smirked as she remained by his side.
"What are you doing, Bruce?" Diana inquired, "Brainiac's track; he left an encrypted code from the previous incident?" "oooh, sounds significant, yeah," he replied flatly.
The bat was too preoccupied with his job to react. Diana was just wandering around aimlessly while whistling. It didn't take long for Batman to get irritated with the large diversion and plan to cancel the study session. He's not seeing much work completed for the Amazon here, "Princess."
She turned to face him as he removed his helm, exposing his grim, brooding, and handsome face that had been buried deep underneath that helm. Diana's heart skipped a beat when his enigmatic black eyes locked on hers.
"Would you like to eat at the Manor?" Diana was shocked to hear his words. Diana's pulse was racing quicker than usual as his eyes on her piqued her interest in the guy himself. She was about to make her move when she recalled Shayera's suggestion, from a female acquaintance, always to play hard to get otherwise, the guy would get the wrong impression.
"Hmmm... Do I know Bruce?" she retorted sarcastically.
Without delay, Batman rose from his stationary chair and switched off the light. His right hand was keeping his helm,

which he had just removed. "Well, have a nice evening then," he said as he turned his back to her and walked forward.

Diana pursued him without delay, wanting to explain what she said. What's the point of playing hard to get if the "guy" isn't willing to play along? The Bat of Gotham is too thick to note in the first place.

"Bruce, don't worry, I was joking. "I'd happily go to dinner with you," she said, a slight smile in her voice. "With me?" " Diana was perplexed for a moment when he posed her a playful question. Bruce was talking to her joining him for dinner, correct? "Yes, with you, that's what you say, right?" she thought to herself. Diana inquired earnestly. "To get somebody to eat with,' Batman didn't even pause to consider a suitable answer as he rambled on about...

"I was hoping to sit at a different place," he joked.

Diana felt a surge of rage rise from her chest to his fist. She couldn't believe his reaction. She was aiming sharp daggers at the guy while his gaze was fixed on the road ahead, a defiant smirk on his face. Suddenly, the Amazon princess devised a brilliant solution to his desperate attempts to elicit a reaction from her.

"I meant I'd like to try Alfred's delectable cooking again. "Hera, you leap to conclusions so easily, Bruce Wayne," she answered with a nervous chuckle, "whatever you say so, princess." "He gave a flat answer.

Diana was much more disappointed after hearing his pathetic answer. He's behaving as though he doesn't think about the dinner or having alone time with her, or he's too dense to realize. Diana was asking him to act like a fool...

He, on the other hand, did not.

They were heading down the corridor towards the teleporter when they came across Flash, who was rubbing his chest, meaning that he was still hungry.

"Hey, boys, where are you all going?" "Wally inquired."

"Splendid! Inner at the Manor," Bruce responded. May I still participate? I've just eaten whip cream afternoon. You don't mind rigging..."

Flash was about to finish his statement when he saw the Amazon give him a look that would frighten perhaps the most terrifying of monsters.

"May I ughhh.." She stared at him again, this time with utmost indignation, and clenched her fist tightly. This made Flash feel so uneasy and anxious that he forgot to react. "You know what, I'll only eat at the cafeteria, seeya," Flash said as he dashed through.

Like a fleeting bubble about to burst, Flash vanished in a heartbeat, leaving each of them stunned. Batman stood there with his eyes narrowed, showing caution, then he looks at Diana, who was turning away and whistling, avoiding meeting the suspicion.

They eventually arrived at the Manor's grand landscape thanks to the teleporter. Alfred then hugged them all. He was shocked to see Diana with him for a split second, but he finally got the hint. Bruce then whispers to Alfred as the butler's eyes open, "Right away, sir," as he dashes into the kitchen.

Diana was then led upstairs by Bruce. Her eyes were fixed on every artwork on the wall that they passed by, and she was overjoyed. She hasn't been here in a long time.

They eventually arrived at their goal. Bruce was anxious to show her the room.

Bruce made his way to the entrance, toggling it open while he danced his hand around the knob. Diana felt both anxious and eager when she realized what she had been fantasizing about for so long. Diana sat on the bed with her eyes closed in suspense as Bruce shut the door.

She was feeling excited, but the idea of actually making love to the guy himself lingered in her mind. Diana is young, but she was able to offer it her all to please him. She was ready to send the Dark Knight her first kiss...

"Take me, Bruce," she murmured.

She opens her eyes to see Bruce Wayne still dressed in full body armor and carrying what seems to be a dress. He had a puzzled look on his forehead.

He mumbled nervously, "Wha..."

"Wait, I guess I misread the whole thing. "So why did he lead me here if not because..." she reasoned. "I guess you missed the whole thing, Princess." " "This is going to be your dressing room, and this is the outfit you'll be wearing," he said quickly.

Diana feels humiliated in a heartbeat. She embarrassed herself in front of the guy, but there was always a way to make it seem like she wasn't considering what he was thinking.

"Oh yeah, uhhh, I was just feeling the overall atmosphere of the place," Diana replied nervously.

"You like this space too much?" he questioned. "Wow," Diana answered with a faint smile as Bruce laid the dress in front of her on the bed, startling Diana for a second. Cheekily, she switched to the garment, stunned at how beautiful it was. She was overjoyed and delighted at the prospect of wearing such a lovely gown.

"It's... It's stunning, Bruce," she said, "and it'd be much more beautiful with you in it..." In hushed tones, he said

Diana became aware of Bruce mumbling to himself.

"Wait, what was that?" She inquired sternly.

"Nothing," he said flatly.

Diana gave him a questioning smile as he turned away, flustered. "I bet this belongs to one of your women, Bruce Wayne," she teased. "It belonged to a lady who I liked," he said.

Diana felt a wave of rage rush at him as she stood corrected to him. When she heard him, she could sense her core tense and her hands clench. It was a prank, and she wanted him to refute it, but...

"What?!?" she yelled angrily.

She listened as his eyes were soft, like a lost little boy's. As he sighed, his face was painted with despair...

"It belongs to my... mum," he stuttered, his voice tinged with sadness.

Diana was feeling guilty as she hugged the dress close to her. Bruce's sad eyes were already drooping to the ground, she found. She could not have leaped to those assumptions, she reasoned.

"I'm sorry, Bruce," she said regretfully. Bruce glanced at her guilty expression as he immediately raised the mood.

"Well, I'm leaving the space now; you wouldn't want me watching, will you?" he joked. Diana gave her a playful smile; her left eyebrow lifted high.

"Anyway," Bruce whispered sharply, "I'll see you at the dinner table."

He softly closed the frame, and with that, he was gone. Diana let out a sigh of sadness as her dreams of seeing him in bed on this lovely night were dashed.

There's always a shot that their date goes well; maybe the Amazon Princess would get her to wish after all. But it is so doubtful that to term it fanciful will be an underestimate.

Diana took the dress and pulled it on in front of the mirror, her shoulders reflected. Her lips curled into a wide smirk as she thought of how their date would go.

Bruce was sitting at the dinner table in his fitted tuxedo and slicked back hairstyle at almost 11 p.m. He was searching his wristwatch for the time while the table trembled from the heavy movement of his left knee. As Alfred poured the martini, he came in and set the wineglass on the table.

Bruce scans his wristwatch again, his left leg trembling more than before, anticipating. The butler noted his strange behavior against this "date" that they'll be getting, and he couldn't help but grin as he saw his unsettled ward.

"Would you like some nuts to calm your jittery attitude, sir?" Alfred inquired.

"Hello, Alfred. Is my hair in good condition?" "It looks splendid, sire," Bruce said nervously. " Alfred replied casually " "What do you think of my suit? Are there any folds or creases?"

"What about my face, facial hair, and brows, sire?" Is there something I've forgotten?"

Alfred then tapped his arm in an attempt to quiet him down. Bruce was just too wound up for a specific dinner date like this one. "You've had dinner with thousands of women before, and none of them had you all worked up like this, sire," he said.

After reading Alfred's terms, Bruce focuses on himself.

"You're right; I suppose I'm really..."

"Relax, sire, and enjoy the night with your lovely lady." "Thank you, Alfred," Alfred said respectfully. "Anytime, Master Bruce,"

Bruce answered when his eye was drawn to someone on the stairwell.

"And speaking about your lovely girl......"

Alfred then spins Bruce around to see the amazing sight that was too beautiful to ignore. Diana was standing on the staircase ahead of them, looking stunning in her black coat, which had once belonged to his mother. The butler then went to the kitchen to prepare the dishes he would cook for this special day and create the intimate atmosphere he had in mind.

Bruce couldn't help but look at the beautiful landscape on the stairs, and each move she took increased his anticipation and nervousness. He was losing his cool in the face of such a graceful object falling from the staircase. Shaken, he could sense his mouth dropping lower by the second as the lady approached him. She tied a lock of her beautiful raven hair behind her neck, making her seem more graceful to him.

He stood up to accompany her beautiful damsel, but each movement he took left him nervous. It didn't help that she was staring at him with a gaze that might melt the ice themselves. To call her enchanting would be an understatement. Diana was almost at the dinner table when Bruce saw her sapphire locks, beautiful face, great lips, curves, all these beautiful things about her that had never been so alluring to him before now.

The stunning lady that had bewitched him from this moment was finally right in front of him, which stunned Bruce for a split second. He collected his thoughts and attempted to form a phrase.

"D-Dia... er, princess..." "Yes, Bruce?" he said nervously. Diana questions in a soft voice, her red lips curving into a sweet grin when she sees a little linen on his neck. She bent in closer to fling it out of his coat, bringing her face up against his. Diana then lifts her head to meet his perplexed expression.

Bruce becomes flustered for a split second, then he turns away at the last second, making a little gap between them. Bruce extends his limb, signaling for her to connect it to hers. It's a kind of gentlemanly gesture. Diana happily accepts the gesture as he leads her to her seat.

"I hope I'm not overdoing it with the dress." He softly muttered, "You look perfect in it," she said.

Passion and intimacy hung in the breeze as they each smiled at each other. They could see their faces leaning together and closer, indicating that the atmosphere had certainly turned to romantic.

"A good evening, Miss Dian," she says abruptly.

As they saw the butler, Alfred came in at an inconvenient moment. "Ok, I'm sorry about the poor timing," Alfred said. "It's okay, Alfred. Back then, you rescued me, "Bruce spoke in hushed tones.

He walked over to his seat, which was on the other side of the four-foot-long table. Diana was ecstatic as Alfred served her the spicy appetizer soup. Diana, overjoyed, inhales the delicious scent emanating from the bowl with a grin that might light up a whole cave. Alfred then proceeded to the other end, where the young master was politely observing Diana eat her appetizer.

"Did we have such an absurdly long table?" "It did have its uses on occasion, particularly when your parents held important meetings with the stakeholders here," Bruce inquired. Alfred reacted angrily.

While listening to the British butler's story, Bruce caresses the table. Even such a table had a long past with his kin...

He then looks to his butler, who has been eagerly waiting by his side for more orders.

"Alfred, thank you for saving my ass. I almost did something that I'll regret for the rest of my life." "You don't need saving, Master Bruce," he said solemnly. Alfred grinned as he wished them both a pleasant evening.

The two of them were the only ones at the long table, so the feeling was a little uncomfortable. The fact that they were too far apart, to begin with, was a major consideration, as was Alfred's intimate atmosphere with the candle lighting and romantic songs, which made it seem like this was more than a simple meal. "Damn you, Alfred," Bruce muttered in his mind.

Diana surveyed the space, admiring the decorations and paintings as she caressed her soup cup. She continued to speak to her about random topics about themselves, and this was such an ideal situation for them to talk about their emotions and such.

"Wow, how I wish this table were even smaller," she mused.

"How's the broth, Diana?" Bruce inquired earnestly.

"Hot, could you please move closer and blast it for me?" she teased.

Bruce was quiet in humiliation, and she laughed softly. Diana frowned, thinking to herself what a waste the setup had been, but what was the point if they were so far apart?

"This is a large table, huh?" she whispered to him. It's where my parents used to dine with their guests." "So it's a guest table for 12 people?" he replied. "That's correct, Diana, you're slowly becoming an investigator yourself," he teasingly said. Diana rolled her eyes and sarcastically uttered, "Duh, I just counted the seats."

Bruce grinned softly as he stood back and watched the lady of the night. He was more at ease now that he knew Diana was indeed Diana beyond her captivating beauty.

He had a feeling all of a sudden.

"Princess, do you want to run out of here?" he asked softly.

"Finally, I was feeling bored here," she said relievedly. Bruce then dashed across the table and towards her. He took her arm and led her to the kitchen, where Alfred was drying the dishes.

"Oh, my word!" "Dinner finished early?" Alfred exclaimed, shocked.

"Anything like that," Bruce said, pulling out a chair for Diana to sit on, along with a special round table designed only for the special guests. They will now chat openly, and they are no longer separated by a long table that creates distance which interferes with their romantic meal. Alfred then arrived with the main course, clam carbonara, and a tempting red wine to accompany it. "Is this kind of dinner appropriate, sire?" While serving the dish, Alfred said to Bruce, "It's okay." Bruce answered with a grin, "Come sit with us, Alfred, tell me stuff about Bruce when he was young." Diana teased Bruce. Alfred chuckled as he took a spot at the roundtable with them. He told her tales of how young Bruce used to climb into rice dispensers and wander around the manor nude. Diana chuckled incessantly, though Bruce stood there feeling ashamed. "After ten minutes, the butler was feeling tired." "It was a nice evening, Ms. Diana, but I'm going to bed now. "Have a blessed evening, Alfred," he said as he walked to his bed. "Thank you, Alfred." "Diana responded

She returned her focus to Bruce, saying, "You were such a naughty kid back in the day, Bruce." "We all were at some stage in our lives," he responded sternly.

Diana yawned, burying her face on her shoulder. The princess seemed to be being more drowsy.

"It's good to know more about you, Bruce, making me realize you're not that heartless at all," Diana joked, tossing her eyelashes at him. "Of course, I have a heart." "Who doesn't," he retorted sarcastically, "but you do have a spirit, Bruce Wayne." I've always suspected you weren't always that grumpy." "I only hesitate to open up to anyone so quickly in case I..." said Diana. "In case you what?" Bruce paused. Diana inquired, giving him a concerned glance. "It's nothing important," Bruce answered, a faint grin on his lips. "Tell me, is this one of the reasons that we can't be together..."

"It's getting late, princess, come I'll accompany you to your space to stay the night," Bruce said, softly taking her arm while she offered him a disapproving glance.

Bruce was escorting Diana back to her bed upstairs at nearly midnight. They had a great time, but all good things must come to an end. The night doesn't last long, and their perfect night had come to an end.

They eventually entered the bed, and Bruce turned to face Diana, who was deep in contemplation. She just stood there and stopped for a few seconds.

"What's the matter, Diana?" he inquired.

Diana was enraged as she turned to face the guy.

"Why do you still avoid discussions like this, Bruce?" she asked quietly. "You have so many to drink; let's call it a night," Bruce said.

"She stared at him with pointed daggers that might scare anybody." "O, you're not going to get away from me again; WHY? Why can't we be together?" "Keep it down, princess; Alfred is sleeping soundly now," he retorted.

Bruce ignored her advances and unlocked the door for her to enter, only to be pulled inside by the Amazon. Diana closed and locked the door from the inside when they were still in the bed." "Now no one can hear us," she raged, "you can't be serious, Diana; you just had so much to drink." Good evening. "He attempted to flee by going to the entrance, but when he turned the handle, he felt a force drag him from behind. Bruce, fortunately, evaded and countered her grip. In a split second, he had her pinned against the wall. "Enough, Diana!" he exclaimed as Diana scrambled to the wall, allowing her to break free. She swept his legs out from under him, causing him to lose his footing and crash for a split second. Bruce attempted to stand but was snagged by the Amazon Princess. His limbs were all pinned on the cement, held back by her godlike might. Diana's hold was so powerful that he couldn't even budge her in the least. When Bruce was once again captivated by her stunning eyes, their faces became too similar to each other. He was sinking deeper and deeper into her sapphire. He could see the statistics stacking up against him despite his inability to do something or even think rationally.

"Please tell me about Bruce." The Amazon spoke with sorrow in her heart, tears welling up in her eyes. Bruce's attention was drawn to the reality that her eyes were now heavy with sorrow and loneliness. He shook his right arm from her grip, cupping his palms to her cheekbones and brushing the tear from her eyes. He whispered to her what he had hoped to express but couldn't for the longest time. He was too reluctant and persistent to let Diana know how he felt.

"It's because..." he stuttered, hesitantly, when Diana's gaze fixed on him.

"I'm... afraid," he murmured in her warped voice.

Diana was taken aback as she heard his words.

"What could the dark knight of Gotham be afraid of?" she said, her voice trembling as tears streamed down her cheeks.

"Hera, it's..." he answered. You single-handedly beat Gotham's most heinous criminals, defeat Vandal by locking away the wand and outwit Darkseid, stopping a global invasion. Bruce, you did all of that without showing any signs of anxiety. YOU DID IT!" Diana screamed angrily, "Now tell me what you're afraid of!"

When he squeezed her two shoulders in front, Bruce saw an opportunity and kicked his leg out to break away from her hold. When she found herself embraced by the man himself, she was too preoccupied with her feelings to protect herself. As he whispered, she could sense his warm breath on her shoulder, "I'm sure I love you a little too much, princess."

Diana couldn't believe what she was about to say. Her face changed to one of surprise. He had just said everything to her that she couldn't imagine. She remained confident that the Dark Knight of Gotham was not in love with her.

She yanked him from his arms and tossed him to the bed. She moved her weight, causing herself to make rapid motions, thus grabbing the lasso off her leg. Bruce realized what was about to happen and managed to break out and flee, but it was too late. He was trapped in her lasso before he had a chance to flee the room. She drew him back and trapped him between the cushions.

"The lasso binds you, and you must confess the facts," she said firmly.

Bruce exclaimed when he realized what was going to happen.

"Do you love me?" she inquired earnestly.

Bruce tried all he could to think of nonsensical thoughts in the hopes of reversing the lasso's effect on him and thereby escaping, but it didn't function. He realized he was shaping a term with his tongue. He tried and tried with every ounce of strength he had left in him before finally...

He relented.

"I love you, Princess," Bruce said.

Diana was delighted to hear such words from him. Since the lasso stops him from lying, he is telling the facts this time."
"Still, I'm afraid of that. I'm afraid I'm going to lose myself because I am obsessed with you. I worry about you all the time, day and night. I can't live by myself, and the fact that I can't have you hurts. I really cannot. We were so different, and I have to understand that, but my feelings come flooding back to your eyes, mouth, curves, and hair every time I see you. Diana, I adore every aspect of you... But we can't be together....."

Bruce admitted when something brushed across his mouth. He was distracted by a romantic embrace from the Amazon princess, who was closing her eyes. When he drew forward, he was already processing all that was going on. Diana blinks open her arms, Bruce rubbing a tear from her lips with one hand while holding her waist with the other. He tucked a strand of her raven hair behind her ear.

"I've always wanted to do that," Bruce smirked.

"I finally had you open, Dark Knight. Now you're all mine. "I was always yours to start with, Diana," she whispered, her voice tinged with pride. He responded with the warmest smile.

"This past month, I'd been longing for some alone time with you, and when you asked me to dinner, I felt joy like no other. I wouldn't want to lose out on the opportunity to be alone with you." "Oh, is that why you gave Wally the glaring daggers earlier?" Diana admitted, to which Bruce responded with a smirk.

Diana grinned seductively as she kissed him again, this time with his palms on the back of his head, mixing up his slicked-back hair.

She drew back and removed her robe, exposing her wonderful body to the man in front of her.

"Diana..." Bruce said hesitantly.

She drew his tie closer to him, their faces tight together, as she sent him a seductive expression of lust. Their lips touched once more as she removed his coat and scarf, slipping her hand to her stomach and finding his scars deep inside.

She ripped apart his dress coat, breaking the buttons in the process. Diana kissed his belly while Bruce sighed with pleasure;

she became more enthralled by his voice as she slid her lips upwards from his neck, his chest, then back to his lips.

Diana hesitated hesitantly, throwing him a malicious smile as he leaned his palms on her hips and slipped down to her buttocks. An expression that resembled a lioness looking at its prey. She moved on to his trousers, removing the belt and pants, leaving just his boxers to cover his broad.

She was taken aback by the scale of his member when she stroked it up and down, making him feel both uneasy and pleasant.

When he felt Diana's warm mouth conquer her, he closed his eyes in ecstasy. With his eyes closed, he sensed a rush come from below as Diana's moans could be heard. It piqued his interest even further, and he bit his lower lip in anticipation. Diana's tongue danced around his rod while her juicy lips squeezed so tightly. He felt for her head while she concentrated on keeping him happy.

"Diana is a formalized paraphrase. I'm going to...

Diana didn't give up when something poured out of every corner of her mouth, accompanied by Bruce's helpless groan of satisfaction, indicating how much pleasure she had brought him. "What is this that you left on my lips, Bruce?" she inquired. "That's my uhh... Seed," Bruce responded while panting. Diana then swallowed every bit of Bruce's liquid from every corner of her mouth. "You didn't have to do that doll," Bruce exclaimed, "but now I have a bit of you in me, forever." She responded with a sweet smile that warmed his heart from inside.

He can't contain himself any longer. The desire that had been following him around for all those days, he fantasized about Diana. Diana chuckled softly as he raised her to his lap. She couldn't believe it was happening, with the guy of his dreams clutching her tightly.

She guided his member to her Amazon cave as he was anxious. "Are you ready, Bruce?" she questioned. "It's my first time, so please be gentle."

"I'm not sure, Princess; we shouldn't be doing this."

Diana rolled her eyes as she silenced him with a kiss that fueled their desire even further. As she moaned enticingly, she could feel the discomfort and gratification emanating from his member.

She can't help but note Bruce's concern about her condition. He was making sure she wasn't in any danger. "Don't worry, Bruce, I love the agony you cause me," she said as she squeezed his head from the front.

Sweat

It was lunchtime at the Watchtower, and the members were having a good time talking to one another. The whole cafeteria was in disarray, with the overarching sound of someone having a good time.

The league has been very active recently, dealing with challenges to the environment that they must address. It will be an underestimate to conclude that today was a difficult day for all of the participants.

But today was different, for they had actually conquered the biggest source behind it all, a man called Vandal Savage. Batman devised a strategy to thwart Savage's scheme to conquer the planet and use its riches for his gain.

The vendetta lasted almost a month, but with the united strength of all the Justice League Association representatives, Savage and his army had little shot.

And now the leaguers will actually relax, knowing that they don't have to think about what's going to come next. They were just having a quiet lunch in the cafeteria.

Clark, Wally, and John were sitting next to each other, laughing and joking about their last task and how it started.

"I knew the guy was behind this all along, Vandal," Flash exclaimed. "Sure you did; I recall you saying that." It was Lex Luthor all along, including the fact that he is now in detention in Metropolis." "I don't know about you, but I'm just happy all of that was eventually done," Superman said. "I will actually have some alone time with Shayera," John said as he ate his cheeseburger.

As they continued their fun chat, Superman and Flash offered him an envious smile.

Diana abruptly joined in and sat down with them. She had just returned from a mission in Egypt, and it seemed the exhaustion was practically painted on her tired face. That task always pushed her to her limits, leaving her exhausted at the end. "Hey Wondy," Wally said spontaneously, "Hi Wally," Diana replied with a faint yawn, "New hairdo?" " John inquired. "It's all the aftereffects of the whole mission. I just returned from a 10-hour trip to Egypt." "That's tough then; you can reach the haystack," Diana said. "Yes, but I'm not sleeping on an empty stomach," John said, to which Diana responded.

They were having a good time with Diana, and Wally was the life of the crowd. Despite her exhaustion, she tried her hardest to have fun with them, but something lacked the ordeal. She was looking forward to seeing someone who might make her happy after a hard day at work. When Clark notices it, she pauses to glance back, checking every table and chair in the cafeteria.

"What's the matter, Diana?" he inquired. "Are you searching for something?"

"More akin to someone..." Flash spoke softly.

Diana frowned at Wally after reading his sly remarks, causing the scarlet speedster to come to a halt in his rambling. She then turned to Clark with a friendly smile as if nothing was wrong. "Ok, I'm only searching for the mixer; it seems like they rearranged the entire cafeteria," Diana replied casually. "Ok, you have Batman to thank for that then," uttered Flash

Wally and John exchanged glances, a smug grin on their lips.

"He's currently distracted, Wondy," Flash said. "Well, you know how glum he can be." John said, "I don't know what you guys are talking about," Diana responded, crossing her eyes, "Sure you don't." Wally sarcastically uttered

Diana became much more enraged; she'd had enough of the scarlet jester, who had turned her even more irritable than before. She was having none of it when she squeezed her cup and attempted to spill it onto Wally, which he managed to dodge with his super pace. The coffee was now going aimlessly in another direction, reaching the individual Diana didn't want to play a joke on.

There he was, The Dark Knight himself, with the same gloomy smile and armor drenched in iced mocha. He twisted his head to look behind him, where the four troublemakers were shivering like a lost puppy in the middle of the lane.

Nobody messes with Batman, and everybody in the league knows it.

"Uh-oh," Flash grumbled.

The entire cafeteria fell quiet while everyone's gaze remained fixed on the occurrence that had just occurred, wondering what might come next.

Bruce yanked a handkerchief from his tool belt and cleaned the iced mocha that was now dripping on his jaw and armor. He walked away with his tray, which had two sandwiches, without making a fuss.

Diana felt terrible as she saw him walk away. At the very least, he was the last one she needed to irritate. She was well aware that she was to blame for the chaos. When it comes to her passions, she loses composure and discipline, potentially working against her. Diana stood up to obey Batman to apologize appropriately, for he was the one who taught her about this. She wasn't going to let the day end without giving them a proper closure about what had just happened. One of the reasons that shaped her into Wonder Woman was her integrity, and accepting errors improves an individual over time. You benefit from your errors and vow never to repeat them. And yet another pearl of insight, this time from the caped crusader himself.

She could only leave the table before she was stopped by Clark, who had a concerned look on his forehead.

"Trust me; you'd just exacerbate the schism while he's angry; give him time," Clark said. "But it was an accident." "Wow, and the only thing you'll get from him is his notorious batglare," she said.

When their dialogue resumed, Diana sat down in sorrow, the same guilty look on her lips. She was too preoccupied with her feelings to attend to their nonsense, so she gave them a determined glance.

"No, this isn't how we Amazons function; I'm no coward, and I will apologize for the error I made," Diana proclaimed as she stood up and dashed to the exit.

The three showed no reaction as they observed her walk forward, her chest raised high like a convict about to embrace her sentence.

Diana went down the corridor, hoping to meet the one she was searching for and apologizing for what had happened. She was well aware of how harsh and intense Batman maybe when enraged, but he didn't care anymore. The last thing she needs is to widen the gap between herself and Batman. She wanted to open up to him rather than drive him further anymore because, after today, she'll have the Caped Crusader all to herself.

"I should've accomplished this sooner if they hadn't held me there." She reflected herself

Diana saw him heading down the infirmary with what seemed to be a towel on his right side. He's more likely going to have a shower.

Diana's mind was quickly consumed with an image of desire as she mumbled to herself about the guy taking a shower. She couldn't help but fantasize about how graceful he is underneath his heavy armor...

Despite the distractions, she kept on her way to apologise to Batman.

Batman entered the infirmary with his wet armor, which had been soaked in iced mocha from earlier. His skin was already damp, and the aroma of caffeinated coffee lingered in his nose.

A certain Amazon Princess was stalking him from afar. Diana pursued him into the hospital and concealed behind the large lockers.

She inhaled and exhaled, trying to gather herself and summon the strength to confront the Dark Knight himself.

She lifted her breasts as she emerged from her hiding place to meet him, only to see Bruce undress with his bareback revealed to her.

Diana couldn't believe what she saw there and held her breath as he removed his helm. She quickly regained her composure when Bruce nearly turned back to find Diana peering at him.

She breathed a sigh of satisfaction when she closed her eyes and pictured how beautiful his body seemed with the sun highlighting his aesthetic muscles.

She became flustered and nervous; this condition was somewhat risky, but she was grateful to be in it. Her pulse was racing at a breakneck rate, and she was sweating profusely.

Diana has never felt anything like this before. She hadn't felt anything as she had while she was with Bruce. She caresses her face as she becomes ever more agitated. The breathtaking landscape she had just seen was too much for her brave yet delicate core to bear. She was a tough princess from a warrior island who had been prepared for battle since birth. This bewitching spell pales compared to the spells she battled for against Circe, but this was different.

She was so preoccupied with a man's naked body. His body, Batman's body...

She caresses her lips as she fantasizes about licking his magnificent muscles: Bruce's chiselled profile, magnificent back, and aesthetically pleasing heart. Diana was too enamoured of him to think rationally.

She yearned for him too much.

As a mischievous grin formed on her cheeks, she covered her mouth with her palm. When she felt hot all over again, a bead of sweat dripped down to her cheek. It was an odd sensation, to be sure, but she didn't mind too much. She was thrilled that he was the one who had bewitched him, a person with a gold heart and the bravery of a thousand men. A man whose power is derived from a will as unbreakable as a diamond.

"He's turned me into this, Hera. Please excuse me for behaving in this manner for a guy, "She prayed quietly.

Her instincts got the better of her when she felt her head turn painfully, but just as she was about to catch that glance, her attention was met by the revealing Dark Knight himself, his arm leaning against the locker while he stared at her with piercing eyes. "Are we having fun?" she wondered, feeling the uncomfortable atmosphere hanging in the air. Bruce said as he stared her in the eyes.

Diana was taken aback when she realized she was stuck in that place, with the man of her dreams encircling her. She was captured in his gaze as if she were not only cornered but still frozen in his gaze. Diana looked as though she was being pulled in more and closer with a smile that could melt even the fiercest of Amazons.

"I'll clarify... I uhh." Diana mumbled apprehensively.

When his hand grasped for something in the locker, he turned his head slightly sideways. Even though Diana realized she was tough enough to smash him against a brick, the entire thing was inconvenient, but she was helpless when it came to those mesmerizing eyes of his.

Diana's legs began to fail her as they began to collapse, and every second she spent alone with him in this space made her tense as she struggled to compose a phrase on the tip of her tongue.

"I just needed to apologize..."

When she opened her eyes, she was distracted by a towel rubbing her cheekbone and the dark knight wiping her sweat from her cheek to her throat. She remained speechless as she saw the guy himself take control of her.

"You're perspiring profusely, princess," he said softly.

Her voice was cracking, and her throat was really dry, and she couldn't say a single sound. Her lips shivered, yearning for something so delectable, and her tongue ached to touch the forbidden mysteries of his mouth.

Diana was so enamoured to even say "thank you," she didn't have the opportunity to apologise to make it understandable, but it looked that he wasn't too upset with what had happened.

"I got you, princess; I will always be here to take care of you," he gently whispered into her ear.

That was the tipping point for her; seeing him name her "princess," she felt as though her eyes blurred, and she was suddenly in a new position with him.

"The Butland," she murmured to herself, referring to a common hangout for her and Bruce. An environment where they will have fun without having to worry about something in the modern world. A spot where nothing could stop them from making love as the moon above illuminated the desire that was building between the two of them.

"Diana," Bruce said quietly. "Be prepared to take your sentence," he says as he pulls her closer to him, his hands caressing Diana's back, making her giggle. Diana couldn't help but shout her eyes to embrace her punishment for being such a sloppy hotheaded kid earlier.

"If this is how my punishment will be every day, I'd happily pour you an iced mocha every day," she teased.

Their lips longed for each other as they got closer and closer. As a strong breeze of the wind of change gently brushes through them, the bright moonlight serves as a witness to the immense passion hovering in the air.

"Bruce... I..." she mumbled.

All she could think of was his name, which was circling in the back of her mind. At the time, he was everything she could think of.

She didn't want someone to wake her up if this was a dream.

"Diana..."

She could hear him say her name, which made him excited because he knows how passionate he can be with her. "Diana..."

The way he pronounces her name is like music to her ears. It seems poetic that such an easy thing he does might elicit such a response from her. "Diana..."

This time, she was a little taken aback, his accent was a little wrong, and his public speech was off. It was as though he were a new guy.

She was interrupted out of nowhere by a voice repeating her name when she heard ambient sounds from a crowd this time. Diana opens her eyes to see herself back in the cafeteria, with Clark, John, and Wally in front of her, waking her up.

The absurdity, the irony, the irony, the irony, the irony

"YoWondy, this spot ain't for sleeping," Wally joked, "may as well grab some pillows and a mattress next time."

"You may want to go to the infirmary, Diana," Clark said. "You were very restless earlier."

"It's okay, I just passed out after all," Diana said, a disappointed expression on her lips before an idea struck her. Her pupils dilated as the idea lingered in her head.

If it was just a fantasy, that says...

"Hello, did Batman come here and..."

"What did I do?"

She turned back to find the guy she had been thinking of standing behind her all this time. She felt so ashamed to even look him in the eyes during her whole dream with him.

"Nevermind," she says nervously.

As the guys were making their way to their headquarters, the bell rang. Diana couldn't imagine she had thought of him again while still remembering what had happened.

"This is the 97th period already," she said to herself, massaging her stressed-out forehead. Diana was quite shaken by what had just happened, but everybody was making their way to their respective quarters.

It didn't take long for her to get up from her seat and head to her quarters to relax after the ordeal of the mission. The one she had before was unsuccessful, and she wished to resume the fantasy she had just had.

She made her way to the gate, intending to go to her respective quarters, when...

"How do you feel, Diana?" Bruce inquired as he approached her side.

She was taken aback when she heard his baritone voice appear out of nowhere. He was dressed in complete armour, his helm concealing his well-proportioned, chiselled features.

"I'm fine, Bruce, just exhausted from the last mission," Diana responded nervously.

Bruce's lips curl into a true humour grin, and he chuckles softly. Diana became aware of the man's unusual attitude all of a sudden. She couldn't help but wonder what had fascinated The Dark Knight himself. "Penny for your thoughts?" she wondered. "What's so funny?" she inquired.

"Must have been a nice dream you were getting there." He responded in a lighthearted manner.

"And what exactly do you mean by that?" "I heard you are moaning my name over and over back there when you were in your deep slumber there," she inquired. Bruce said with a smug grin on his lips.

Bruce was assertive because he realized Diana was probably thinking of him. This amused him quite a little. Diana came to a halt as she heard his words; she stopped in the corner, her tongue clenched deep in her mouth. She wanted to explain what it used to be. Otherwise, he'd get the wrong impression.

"The letter I-

"It's not as it seems to be!" she said nervously, a distressed grin on her lips. "Sure it is, but you may want to wash the sweat off your face." You were sweating profusely earlier, "Bruce said as he walked away in a separate direction.

Diana had a playful smile on her face when she apprehended him.

"Wait, Bruce," she said cautiously.

When he heard her call his name, he turned to face her. When she asked him, she had a seductive mischievous grin on her mouth...

"Would you like to accompany me to the infirmary to assist me in wiping all over?"

The Late-Night Get-Together

Bruce stood in front of Diana's bedroom, waiting for her to open the gates. Diana looks through the peephole and sees a guy in a nice suit with a bouquet. Bruce stumbles upon seeing her, and she answers the bell.

"Wow, it took a long time," he exclaimed.

"Oh, quit it, a lady has to look beautiful now and then," she responded with a sly grin.

Bruce Wayne takes up a flower from the bouquet and tries to reach out towards Diana's face but pulls back at the last second. Diana is perplexed; she was anticipating a pass from Bruce Wayne. She looks at him, disappointed, and expects him to make the first step because his Dark Knight is too timid.

"Let's get started, Diana," Bruce said.

"Say, Bruce, how do I look in my dress?" she inquired, her eyes gleaming.

Bruce gives her a hesitant smile. His thoughts were jumbled as he attempted to shape a compliment or something similar.

"You look..." Bruce whispered hesitantly, "Yessss?" Diana inquired, bending in closer to see his face.

"You look...... properly groomed for the moment," Bruce remarks as he strides on.

Diana has a major pout on her face when she smiles at him. She was also more dissatisfied by the reality that she had spent over six hours preparing and had just received half-hearted praise.

Bruce realizes he's already carrying the peach gladiolus flower he was holding earlier and decides to conceal it in his suit. As Alfred welcomed the lovely Amazon Princess in her stunning nightgown, he led Diana to the limo. "A nice evening, Miss Diana," Alfred respectfully greeted.

Diana responded with a smile as she boarded the limousine.

He then drove them to the museum, where a stakeholder group was being organized. Bruce seemed to be worried about everything, so it was a long quiet journey. They came to a halt at a red traffic light.

As Alfred notices Diana fixing her skintight black coat, she stares in the rearview mirror.

"You look particularly lovely today, Miss Diana," Alfred says, and Diana looks back at him in the rearview mirror.

"Thank you, Alfred; unlike a certain other, you genuinely respected and congratulated me. Isn't that true, Bruce?" Diana made an obnoxious remark as she turned to face Bruce, who was gazing out the window at the view beyond.

Diana scowls and folds her arms to her side as she turns away. Alfred observes the young master in the rearview mirror, noting the difference between them.

Bruce returns Alfred's grim look from the same mirror as Alfred nods in Diana's direction, signalling for Bruce to make a pass. Bruce frowned, attempting to shape a phrase under his breath, "Diana..."

Diana sees Bruce and smiles at him.

"Yes?" she inquired slowly.

She steps up to him when she tries to peer into his eyes, but he tries to avert her glare.

"You look......," he said hesitantly, "Yes....?" Diana inquired politely as she drew closer to the unsettled Bruce.

When he actually caught Diana's attention, he became much more flustered and tongue-tied. With Diana so tight, he clenches his hand.

"You take a peek......"

He was about to say the following words when he noticed a loud tapping from the driver seat doors. It was a scruffy guy with a

Glock on his right side and a purse in his back. As the man aimed the pistol at the butler, Alfred opened the doors.

'Don't make any needless moves; send me all you have, including money, credit cards, wristwatches, and jewellery.'"

Diana was bracing herself for a battle when she realized Bruce's cool response.

"Why isn't the Batman himself interested in what's going on?" she wondered.

Diana's emerald chain dangles around her ear, and the man sees it.

"You girl, hand me those necklaces right now!" he screamed angrily.

Diana became much more enraged when Bruce took her hand to cool her down. "He's got this," Bruce said quietly, "He?" Diana inquired, her voice trembling.

The guy became irritated with their conversation and aimed the pistol at Diana, leaving him free for a counter-attack. Alfred lost little time in disarming the guy with a quick punch to the gut. Alfred stabbed the man's jaw from the side, grabbed his shoulder, and hurled him to the deck, causing him to groan in agony.

"If only you knew what you disrupted, you inconceivable rodent," Alfred yelled angrily[1].

The guy stood up and steadily took a knife from his pocket.

"Look, just send me the car, and I'll take you all away," he said.

Alfred pops his knuckles and laughs.

"How daring of you to think you'll get away with the odds stacked against you," Alfred answered as he easily disarmed the guy with his knee stuffed to the man's back, forcing him to kneel in front of the butler.

When Bruce interrupted, Alfred took out a taser to completely knock him out of his pain. "We'll be late, Alfred," Bruce said roughly.

"Right now, sire," Alfred said as he returned to his motorcycle. "Besides, I'm sure I'll make him see sense later tonight." "Of course you can," Bruce said with an evil grin on his lips. Diana let out a short chuckle. Suddenly, an idea came back to her.

"Anyway, Bruce, what were you going to say earlier?" Diana inquired.

Bruce glanced at her, noticing Diana's interest in him. "Oh, it was nothing substantial," Bruce said flatly, sitting on her arms with her legs pointing towards him.

Diana was dissatisfied with his answer. "Fine, hold your secrets," Diana answered resentfully.

Alfred takes another glance at them in the rearview mirror. They were back to where they were before, with the whole distance and the tense atmosphere. As the Butler frowned, Bruce looked at him in the mirror, concerned.

XX

They've arrived at their goal, only to see paparazzi waiting for them outside. Bruce was the first to leave, and he was met with photo flashes and inquiries from the media waiting outside. He moved to the other side of the vehicle to unlock the door for Diana, only to be slapped in the face by her opening it herself. "I am sure of how this operates, Mr Wayne," she said angrily.

She marched alone through the door while the photographers and paparazzi surrounded her. They remembered who she resembled now; it was Wonder Woman.

They quickly barraged her with questions and video flashes. For a brief second, she staggered, blinded by the lights that were overwhelming her view.

"Miss Wonder Woman, what takes you to Gotham?"

"Wow, I'm only here for a tour," Diana said, smiling. "How do you know Mr Wayne?"

As she heard the comment, she turned to Bruce, who was chatting with Alfred about something. "Oh, we weren't together," she said. Diana said it louder enough that Bruce, of all people, could understand it.

She proceeded to waltz indoors, perplexing Bruce with her abrupt mood swing. "What's the matter, Alfred?" he said, turning to Alfred, who was suppressing a slight chuckle. "Oh, I think Miss Diana is very distressed about something," Alfred responded as Bruce glanced at her as he walked cautiously to the door.

"She's not going to go in without me; that's why she's accompanying me." Bruce scoffed. Alfred is worried as he looks at her.

Bruce entered the museum, ignoring any of the reporters' concerns. He immediately went in pursuit of a certain obstinate lady who simply refuses to follow the scheme. He sees a crowd gathered in one place, which is most likely where she was. He dashed to the scene, and, as he had expected, Diana was in the centre, unsettled by the people hounding her with queries. He pulled her out of the crowd and into a corner by grabbing her arm in the centre.

"Many thanks for coming to my help."

"What on earth do you think you're doing?" Bruce demanded angrily, "I'm uhhh..."

"We've discussed it; we need to stay together in the group; otherwise, they'll find that we're after anything other than the fossils. I'm warning you that if you don't behave appropriately, this project will fail spectacularly."

"You are not the boss of me, Batman, and you would not rob me of being myself or how I should behave on those festive occasions," Diana brushed his grip on her and sent him a furious glare. "Diana, we're not here to have a good time. The league has organized a recon operation to intercept individual stakeholders that might have links to the latest smuggling of heavy kryptonite. "Well, this isn't what I signed up for, Batman," Bruce protested sternly.

Bruce saw a guy staring at them suspiciously as the Amazon was rambling about something.

"Hello, Diana! Stop acting like a kid and get your act together; darn it. "Were you even listening?" Bruce demanded angrily. Diana demanded angrily, "There are suspicious men the..."

Bruce didn't even finish his sentence before being slapped hard by the Amazon, which drew a lot of interest in the museum when Diana dashed away from him. Bruce kept his composure with his happy arrogant grin and headed over to a vacant corner where few people. He activated his communicator earpiece." "We can't sit here, Alfred; they've been assigned to us. She's sabotaging the scheme, and I'm the one who has to clean it up." Bruce murmured, " "That may be the case; what do you want to do now? " Alfred responded through the earpiece " "or I'll go for plan B for the time being. I still had enough information about these individuals last night to figure out what they're after, and it turns out my assumptions were right all along." "Is that so? I'll begin the atmosphere scanning now for some distractions in the group that could trigger any mishaps," Bruce said quietly while scanning the space for someone eavesdropping. "Please do, Alfred, and update me afterwards," Alfred responded. Bruce said as he removed his earpiece.

Someone from Behind approached him unexpectedly.

"Are you having a band, Mr Wayne?"

He turns back to see Lucius Fox, who is dressed well in a fitted coat.

(Lucius Fox is a near friend of Bruce Wayne's.) He is an accomplished businessman, entrepreneur, and designer who unwittingly runs the business interests that provide guns, gadgets, cars, and armour for Bruce Wayne to use as the superhero Batman while fighting crime. He is one of the few individuals that recognize Bruce Wayne as Batman.)

"What brings you here, Lucius?" "I know what's going to happen, Mr Wayne, and I have something that could pique your curiosity," Bruce inquired enthusiastically. With a smile, Lucius responded.

Bruce glanced around again, looking for something unusual. Lucius sees his cautious attitude and chuckles, "Master Wayne, even in a fine suit, you are Batman after all." According to Lucius

Lucius escorted Bruce to the parking lot where his van was located. He opened the trunk of the van's storage to show the billionaire what he'd been up to these past months." "r. Wayne, allow me to introduce you to the most recent edition. Your most recent outfit," Lucius started boldly, but Bruce was not impressed by the costume. It seemed to be identical to his new one, although a little is less bulky.

"What is the most recent? This one is identical to my new one. What's the deal for this one?"

"Ah, Mr Wayne, that's where you're mistaken." Lucius boasted as he pressed a button on his bat suit, rendering it translucent.

Bruce couldn't believe his eyes as they seemed to disappear right in front of him.

"For a long time, my team has been fascinated by refraction and how light bends in particular ways. What used to be unlikely is rendered possible by a metamaterial cloth. Without the need for many projectors and sensors, metamaterials have a more clear view of invisibility technology." Lucius narrated with concern.

"Not only that, but our researchers discovered silk that is solid and resilient enough to withstand specific injury. This silk is derived from improved spiders housed in our testing facilities. They've developed silks that can withstand serious stress and harm from external threats such as machine guns if I can continue....." "It is very enticing Lucius, what are you on about?" Lucius continued. Bruce says emphatically, " "Mr Wayne, I'm asking you. This level of control is unfathomable for a single person."

When he shifts to face the armour, Bruce nods smugly to his terms. He was very pleased with the suit that Mr Fox showed to him. When he turns to face Lucius, he curves his lips into a completely optimistic smirk.

"Is it available in black?"

Lucius chuckled as he poked Bruce on the back. They were having a nice time until his communicator beeped out of nowhere, "What's the status, Alfred?"

"Excuse me, sire, but Lex and all his men have already left just now."

"Good, Alfred, make sure you trace them."

"That'll do, sir. So, what are you going to do now?"

Bruce glances at his wristwatch, remembering just what he has to do.

"There's always plenty of time until the party finishes Alfred, I'll go socialize for a while," Bruce answered as he shut off his communicator. "They've evacuated since watching my date coming in," Bruce boasted. "Wonderwoman, not poor Mr Wayne," Lucius said when he opened the car door. "Safe to say you won't need the suit for tonight then." " "Precisely, I'll send you more days to paint it black," Lucius seemed to ask. Bruce responded.

Lucius grinned as he climbed into the car seat.

"Good evening, Mr Wayne," As he rode past Bruce with the Van holding the costume, Lucius confirmed that the Batman will be more threatening from now on.

Bruce stood there watching the van float away in the parking lot until an idea struck him. As he flipped on his communicator "Alfred," he developed a crooked grin on his mouth.

"Yes, sire, is there a problem?"

"Not really; I really require your assistance with everything." As he stepped back into the museum, Bruce exclaimed, "Is it safe to assume that tonight's goal is jeopardized?"

"Not today," Bruce said XX.

Diana stood on the balcony, mesmerized by the moving cars and the enticing lights that sparkled brightly in the darkness. She was also irritated that Bruce regarded tonight as nothing more than a routine assignment when she had foolishly expected that their friendship would undoubtedly change after tonight.

She gazes at the stars, illuminating the sadness she harbours in her core, aware that her feelings for Batman himself grow deeper with each passing day.

"Oh Hera, grant me the courage to survive this feeling I have with him," she prayed quietly, a tear forming in her cheek. "Nice evening, huh?"

A voice breaks her solemn moment when she sees the one she's been praying for standing by her side, gazing at the same stars.

"How can you do that all the time?" "That's my secret princess," she said intriguingly. Bruce responded with a sly grin on his mouth.

She gives him a puzzled look before bursting into a full laugh, but then she remembers something...

She was supposed to be upset with him.

"You're so secretive, and it irritates me so much; I wish you would reveal something about yourself often," she turned her face in the other direction, her arms crossed in her stomach. Diana responded angrily. Bruce gives him a mocking glare and steps closer to her. "Diana..." "If you come here just to prattle about how I'm unsociable and unpresentable, you're just going to make me angrier," Bruce said slowly. She sassed Bruce.

Diana rolled her eyes at him, giving Bruce her familiar galled look.

"Are you planning on entertaining your corporate partners?" "Nah, doing stuff like that gets boring finally," he said, and Diana chuckled a little as she turned to him, and her hatred towards him vanished.

"What were you doing here by yourself in the first place?" "I'm going to brood, much as you still do," he inquired. Diana teased him with a sly grin.

"You're getting it wrong, Princess," Bruce says with a laugh. "Is that so?" he asked, to which she replied.

When a gust of wind blew in, there was a brief uncomfortable pause between them. Diana closed her eyes in delight as the cool breeze caressed her skin.

She looked over to the man beside her and noticed he was doing the same thing she was.

Diana's lips curved into a grin when she realized she was looking into him. It was as though she wasn't looking at the formidable Dark Knight. This version of him isn't threatening at all; in fact, he reminds her of a boy.

He slowly raised his eyes and turned to face Diana, who was staring at him.

"Is there something on my face?" he inquired quietly. "Yes, there is." She teased him once more, this time with a mischievous smile on her lips. "Yeah, you have an expression on your face that's so not you," he inquired. "Wow, how dare you" "I honestly didn't want to be joined by the friendly and vibrant Bruce Wayne when we entered the museum." "He teasingly responded, and then the same quiet filled the whole vibrant mood that they had only seconds before. Diana's gaze was drawn to the man beside her, who was deep in contemplation. "D-Diana.." he whispered, "yes?.." She responded slowly. He seemed as though he was about to tell her something private or intimate. Diana became ecstatic all of a sudden.

"I'm sorry for bossing you around earlier and ordering you how to behave and dress to be presentable," he admitted.

"Aww, the Dark Knight is actually admitting his mistakes?" she said. "I've learned, there's no point in making you into something presentable...b-because you still look dashingly stunning yourself," he said hesitantly.

Diana was stunned for a split second. Is she sure she understood what she just heard? The Dark Knight, above all nations, praising her!

"I didn't quite hear what you were doing, Bruce; what were you doing?"

"Nothing," he says. Bruce responded in a monotonous speech.

He returned to his Batman voice and speech. This irritated Diana once again; she was certain of what she had learned and needed to hear it again.

"Oh, Bruce, say it again."

"No" "Pleaseeeeeeeeeeeeeeeeeeeeeeeeeeeeee

"Oh come on, Bruce, don't be such a snob," I exclaimed, "I figured you came here to be just like me." As he bent in closer to her, he teasingly responded with a subtle smirk on his face that looked so assured and alluring.

Diana turned to find the guy of her dreams standing right next to her, holding her breath. His fragrance is like an irresistible opioid that draws her ever closer to him. She blinked her eyes together in suspense. She collected her thoughts and opened her eyes, only to see his profile ever closer.

"What's the matter, princess?" "You're being......," he teased.

Bruce caressed her face as she mumbled something. "I'm what?" he gently whispered to her ear as her warm breath caressed her neck.

His touch instantly jolted her nerves. It left her so crazy and jumpy on the inside that her lips shivered with enthusiasm. She yearned for him too much.

"B-Bruce..... I'm..." she stammers nervously.

She saw his hands steadily slipping down to her majestic curves as she gazed at him with intense passion. Throughout it all, his gaze never left hers, and she could sense the heavy mood that was in the breeze.

"I have something for you..." he said to her as he took the same flower he had earlier taken from his coat and put it on her left ear.

When he fixes a lock of her raven hair behind her neck, he steps forward, putting some space between them.

"There, you look much more stunning now," Bruce said calmly.

Diana was rendered speechless. It was as though I were in a dream. Hera then gave her wishes based on all the nights she thought of him and how much she wished to think about him some more. The words of the Dark Knight himself lingered in her mind, and she felt ecstatic on the inside.

"Something about me, I like powerful people that are feminine and graceful," Bruce said softly with a charming smile.

The way he spoke those words turned her bright red all of a sudden. When she touched the herb, her heart pounded quicker than normal. She grinned subtly when she caught sight of him gazing at the stars.

"The vision is really lovely from here," Bruce remarked, amusement on his face. Diana responded calmly.

Diana was too preoccupied with a certain someone to see the stars.

The Nighttime Tale

Diana had been in her quarters for almost 30 minutes, lying in her bunk. The Amazon Princess had a long day today since she was tasked with a one-day assignment in Egypt. She wanted a full night's sleep, but for some reason, she couldn't sleep.

She was looking aimlessly at the walls, recalling childhood memories. As her mother, Queen Hippolyta, read her beautiful fairy tales about the realm of men. She closed her eyes and smiled as she sought to recall her mother's beautiful stories.

It was already late, and for some reason, I couldn't sleep; I wanted to practice more and more. I cautiously rolled out of bed and tiptoed to the exit, hoping to get out as the door slowly creaked open. It was, of all people, my mother!

"Hello, Diana. What are you thinking, young lady?"

My mother asked me to look away when I hid my bracelets behind my back.

"I just needed to get some fresh air, Mother," I admitted hesitantly.

My mother sent me a questioning glance. There was no way to fool the queen of Themyscira, and I knew it. She approached me, nodding, and softly caressed my hair.

"Diana, you've used this excuse too many times; did you really believe that would fit for your mother?" she said a playful smile on her mouth.

I had a feeling! There's no chance I will fool my mother; she's much too intelligent and astute for all of my devious misbehaviour. I gently waltz back to my bed, praying she won't be too upset. She shook her head in surprise, my mother had always been compassionate with such a stubborn daughter like me, and I am grateful to her for putting up with me.

Mother perched beside me on the bunk, softly pinching my cheeks.

"Would you like to hear a bedtime story, Diana?" merrily proposed she

Can I do it? Bedtime tales are fantastic! I hear lovely stories and tales of princesses, fairies, romance, romance, romance.

"I'd adore that mum!" I responded in a flurry of excitement.

She started slowly with her typical "Once upon a time..." as I stared at her with curiosity. I adored my mother's voice; it was so full that every phrase she spoke rang true through my heart. I closed my eyes and pictured the tale she was telling.

"Tonight's tale is about a kind and compassionate girl who was humiliated by her second family, but she remained honest and real in the face of all the difficulties life threw at her. One day, the King declared that a royal ball would be held in the castle tonight and that every fair maiden in the kingdom would be welcomed. The girl was overjoyed at the news, but her wicked stepmother prevailed. She screamed and cried all night in her crib, losing hope of entering the crowd, until unexpectedly a fairy godmother stood before her!"

"Does she have a fairy godmother?" " I inquired, my curiosity piqued." "A fairy godmother, if you like. She provided the girl with all she wanted to have a good time for the evening.

However, there is some disappointing news. When the clock strikes midnight, she reverts to her old self. The girl was not disappointed because she had already been rewarded with the Fairy godmothers' present to her, and she immediately set out for the ball. She was the most stunning of them all as they arrived at the palace, even the others could say. When he purposefully approached her, the Prince spotted her from a mile away. As the music begins, he invites her to a party.

They danced gracefully, with the girl enjoying the moment. It felt like a prophecy had come true!

The Prince inquired about her identity, and just when she was about to say it, the large clock rang.....

It was already noon!

Fixated, she dashed for the exit, leaving his prince charming befuddled, and unknowingly left her glass slipper behind when she fled. She arrived at their house with a big grin on her face; this night had been absolutely magical for her.

The following morning, she was awoken by a noisy trumpet signalling the arrival of the royal family. She dashed downstairs, where the king and prince were frozen in place. They tried the glass slipper on every lady in the kingdom to see who it would match, but it didn't, at least not yet.

When the prince saw the child, he sensed something deep inside him. He had to admit to himself that this..... was her.

He took the slipper and put it on the kid, and it was a perfect match! He was well aware of it.

The Prince then arranged for a lavish wedding for them.

And they all lived happily ever after..."

"Forever after," I reasoned.

I was giggling to myself as I remembered how all of my mother's tales ended on a happier note, with the prince and princess living happily ever after. I, too, wished to live happily ever after with a prince.

"Dear Mother, Do you think I'll meet my Prince Charming soon?" I inquired.

Mother gave me a sad expression. As she whispered the terms, she caressed my hair "y youngster; These tales are just that: tales. There are men out there that are too shallow to recognize a girl's value. Diana, Prince Charming does not happen in real life. "I couldn't believe it as she quietly whispered, "I'm heartbroken." What makes her so certain of men and what they're made of? That can't be real, can it?

"However, mum..." "I responded hesitantly. "In dreams, everything is probable, Diana. That's the allure of it." "Fantasies?" Mother said.

"Yes," she said.

Mother kissed my forehead goodnight as she got up. "Goodnight, Diana," she said as she walked out. I gently bundled myself in the fur blanket and closed my eyes. Oh, how I wish I could find my prince charming really quickly.

Diana opened her eyes when she heard a tap on her bed.

"It's me, Diana."

It was the voice of a god. A voice that, for some reason, made Diana really happy. She could tell who it was only from the sound of his speech.

Diana responded in a nice tone, "come in."

The door didn't even flutter, and there was no answer at all. Diana waited patiently, but there was no answer, even though she welcomed him in. Suddenly, a woman spoke up...

"Are you still naked?"

"What exactly do you mean?" Diana responded with a sly grin.

"The last time we played this scene, I saw something I shouldn't have done."

"Oh, Bruce, quit squabbling and just come in," Diana said somewhat irritably.

As Batman entered, the door shifted subtly as he held a cup of barley tea. As he looked around her bed, he put it on her table. His gaze was anywhere but hers. "Take a snapshot; it'll last longer," he said. She tasted enticing.

Batman finally turned to look at her as he carefully set the teacup on her desk.

"I'm sorry, it's been months since I've been here." He gave a detailed answer.

Diana's attention was drawn to him, and she offered him her trademark teasing look.

"You're invited to drop in at any moment." "It's not like I'll mind..." she said casually.

"How did the mission go, Diana?" he inquired harshly.

When Bruce heard that, he quickly changed the subject. This style of discussion will potentially contribute to something dangerous. He sure did save a really personal bullet there.

Diana stood up straight, her back against the headboard of the bed. "Very tiring really, my body is already exhausted after a hard day," she said. He responded monotonously, "I see," she replied.

Diana was already looking at the worried Dark Knight, but there was an uncomfortable pause between them. "Thank you for coming to see me, Bruce," she said with a sincere grin on her mouth. She said it sincerely.

Bruce becomes humiliated all of a sudden. He knew he came here to check on Diana, but it seems she had the wrong impression about his intentions. After a hard day on the mission, he wanted to explain his goal when he went to her quarters. In these scenarios, everyone will have the wrong idea. Diana's sweetness just adds fuel to the flames. Bruce was well aware that he ought to save the atmosphere from deteriorating into something unprofessional, such as affection.

"Anyway, I made you some barley tea, which is great for soothing your muscles. Since it is still hot, I suggest consuming it as soon as possible, "Bruce said while referring to the cup of barley tea she had put on her desk.

Diana leaned in closer to him as he did his typical "professional" Batman pass. That didn't go well with her.

"Can't you, at the very least, remove your helm while you're in my room? I can't take you seriously while you're worried about your whole Batman character, "Diana jokingly said

He shifts his gaze to her, bending in closer. If this continued, it was clear that it might turn terrible at any time. For whatever explanation, she was pushier today than in previous days. He wanted to avoid it until they did something they would later regret." "Anyway, that's all there is to it. Diana, have a nice night's sleep." "Bruce, wait...?" Bruce said as he got up and attempted to quit. Diana uttered in a sad tone. Bruce turned around hesitantly, "What's wrong?" he inquired. Diana was fidgeting her fingers nonchalantly, clearly wanting to say something but too shy to speak up. "Diana?" Bruce inquired some more.

"Bruce, I'm having difficulty sleeping." Bruce grinned and shook his head when Diana murmured in a rather shy way. "Alright, princess, how can I help?" he said as he removed his helm and sat with her on the bunk. According to Bruce

Diana turned around to see The Dark Knight unmasked, his handsome and brooding face revealed to her. For whatever explanation, it left her jumpy and excited. She wanted nothing more than to touch his lips with her own. "When I was a child, my mother used to tell me bedtime stories to make me fall asleep."

Sincerely, Bruce said

Diana's eyes gleamed out of nowhere, signalling that thought had struck her. "That's all there is to it! Say me a bedtime tale, Bruce ", she exclaimed with zeal

"Do you think you're too mature for the Princess?" With a small laugh, he remarked, " "Come onnnnnnnnnnnnnnnnnnnnnn Please, please, please, please, please, please, please, please, please, please, please" Diana begged like a kid.

As he saw this version of the Amazon princess, Bruce couldn't help but laugh. She's behaving like a kid. This image of her is so cute. "OK, but you have to drink your milk first," Bruce joked.

Diana shifted her gaze to the Barley tea he had set on the table. "Well, we have our milk right here," Diana joked.

"Wait, are you sure you're doing this?" He inquired anxiously, "of course we are," Diana responded.

Diana sipped her barley tea as she waited for the tale to begin. She laughed for a split second when she felt relieved all of a sudden. Given the fact that she had had a difficult day, her body seemed to be soothed.

"Wow, this is absolutely magical, Bruce," she exclaimed in awe. Bruce came up with a brilliant plan to divert her attention. This is an excellent opportunity to divert the princess's attention away from the immature proposal she is proposing for him to do.

"Of course, the barley tea is produced from..."

"Please tell me the plot!" Diana cut in, a subtle smile on her lips. This time, it didn't fit.

Bruce, recognizing he couldn't charm his way out of this, agreed to simply follow. As a result, the bedtime tale starts.

"Once upon a time...," says the narrator. He started quietly.

Diana was so engrossed in the tale that she was resting on her hands when he began to tell it.

"So, there was a princess once upon a time. She was stunningly gorgeous, powerful, and intellectual. She essentially had everything."

Diana was admiringly listening to Bruce's account. She had no idea Bruce was a fantastic storyteller.

"She had always decided to discover the universe, so she quit her empire and set off for an expedition around the world, but her mum, the queen, wasn't happy, but that didn't deter her."

Diana found that the princess had an uncanny resemblance to her. This piqued her curiosity in Bruce's story even further.

"On her way, she was followed by a knight." The knight was dependable and trustworthy, and he went to great lengths to shield the princess, despite the fact that he recognizes she is tough enough to support herself."

Diana was piqued as she heard the following parts. She closed her eyes and imagined everything in his head.

She grinned quietly to herself, thinking to herself, "A knight, huh?"

She closed her eyes and imagined everything in his head. She pictured herself as the princess and the knight as the Dark Knight himself.

"On their trip, they encountered difficulties. However, they met them... together, and so they stood firm despite all odds."

Diana was curious about where this tale was heading. "Eventually, the knight felt something different about her, something unexplainable and new," she said, feeling very calm and solemn as she listened to his rich and mystifying expression. He recognized that he was falling in love with the princess.

Diana was having a great time in that story. "She understood who Bruce was referring to with the knight now." Still, alas, the knight had known all along that they weren't meant to be. He was just a..... warrior, and she was a Princess.

"Oh, please!" Diana screamed unexpectedly.

When Bruce saw Diana was still up, he exclaimed, "I thought you were already sleeping!" I didn't like how the plot turned out, so fix it!" "But why?" Diana questioned. "It's just a lie." "But..." Bruce responded logically. "You'd like the conclusion of the novel, believe me," she mumbled. "All right..." Bruce said with a grin. Diana spoke hesitantly.

"So one day, the princess encountered a charming Prince who had everything a woman might desire," she took a drink of the barley tea as she waited for the continuation. She followed him, and they lived happily ever after. "This is the finish."

Diana frowned at her storyteller, clearly dissatisfied with the story. That wasn't the ending she had hoped for. Bruce looked at her, visibly perplexed, "what's wrong?" "Didn't you like the story?" "Not," Bruce inquired. Even a smidgeononononononononononononon "But why, isn't that how most fairy tales end?" Diana scowled. "Are the princess and Prince Charming going to get married at the end?" He also added

Diana was irritated with what he did. She squeezed her hand and stared at him evermore.

"No, that's not the story I was hoping to tell." I didn't like how the story ended; in reality, I hate it." "Ok, then, how would you like to finish it?" Diana protested furiously.

"The Princess and the Knight are destined to be together." She responded in a lighthearted manner.

Bruce shook his head in surprise, "You know darn well that's now how most tales will finish; the Princess and the Prince Charming ended up being the most believable," he said convincingly.

Diana became much more annoyed after hearing how irrational he seemed as a thought occurred to her.

"Well, Bruce, you don't have to be truthful." "What do you mean?" she asked. "In fairy tales, everything is probable," he responded. "And that holds in this situation as well," she added convincingly, "b-but..."

Diana turned to look at him with puppy eyes as he tried to come up with an explanation "Bruce... please." She pled earnestly, and Bruce relented. Let's just give the princess everything she wants. In any case, this is all a dream.

"Fine," he said, and Diana was overjoyed. She easily drew herself back into her blanket, eagerly hoping for the happy ending she craved. She closed her eyes and formed a grin on her mouth.

"So one day, the knight collected all his bravery to inform the princess how he feels," Bruce said. Despite understanding how risky it is to be around someone like him, that was riddled with darkness... Despair...misery... and... sorrow.

For a brief moment, Diana was concerned that Bruce was getting too intimate with the plot. And in his dreams, the Mysterious Knight remains the same as he is with his whole secretive and dark character. "Despite all of that, the idea of residing with the lady he loved the most is the greatest thing that he will ever have in existence." As a result, he told her how he feels. " Diana's concerns were heard. "The Knight had the confidence to tell the princess how he feels considering all the things that were holding him apart... It was really genuine and impressive to her." And so, to his delight, it turned out the princess loved him back. He was unquestionably the greatest guy on the planet at the time," Bruce added.

Diana was pleased to be speaking to him; it seemed real and sincere. "So both of them lived happily amid all the difficulties and disasters that might have fallen their way." They'll be powerful if they work together. And they all survived."

"And they lived happily ever after..." Diana mused to herself before falling asleep with a sincere grin on her lips.

When Bruce realized his princess was still sleeping, he turned to her. He felt content on the inside, feeling that at least in his dreams,... they were together.

Bruce kissed her on the cheek before leaning in tight to say something into her ears.

"Princess, good night..."

He stood up to leave the bed, leaving her Amazon princess in her most relaxed slumber with the cutest smile on her face.

Ace the Bat-Wingdog

"Nearly there... and over."

I mutter to myself as I spill Ace's food for the day into his tiny bat tub. Unlike the other puppies, he doesn't consume much for some purpose that remains a mystery, if I might presume.

The Manor has been unusually quiet recently, owing to Tim's involvement with the Teen Titans and Barbara's attendance at work. It's not because I'm not used to living alone; it's just...

This home is much too big for Alfred and me...

I was muttering to myself as I heard the door creak open. It was Alfred with what seemed to be a cloche on an usher board with a bottle of martini and the Lemon hanging by the corner. "Dinner will be served momentarily, sire," he said, "I better set the dinner table for the master's supper." "Alright, Alfred, I'll be there," Bruce said.

Alfred turned to look at the puppy, whose tail was caressing his shoulder. Smiling to himself, he patted Ace on the back, and the hound surrendered fully, rolling on the other side and revealing his belly.

"What an athletic puppy," Alfred exclaimed, "such a shame, his appetite is contradictory." "Indeed," I reply flatly, "do you suppose we can call a veterinarian for his health, sire?" "It's not that he's been lethargic or passive," Alfred inquired. He just doesn't chew as much as the other puppies." "Very good, sire," I said, turning to face the door with the cloche.

Thoughts raced through my mind as I noticed Ace's demeanour; he's not ill or something, but something is off about the way he eats. Being the brilliant investigator that I am, I would be pretty useless if I couldn't get to the root of this.

In the Batcave, with the general gloom that was engulfing the whole building. For some excuse, I found myself typing into the Batcomputer the triggers of dog appetite loss. It has been a long and difficult trip to find solutions to such a ludicrous situation. Is it possible for me to use the Brother Eye for such a ridiculous reason?

I was so engrossed in my thinking that I didn't hear the noise from the communicator; it was Alfred.

"Sire, will you please come to the living room?" Alfred asked over the communicator. "You have a visitor waiting."

"I'm busy, Alfred. Send them on their way." I reply sternly, "It's obviously just some reporter in every case." I'm certainly not in the mood to address any questions or to be in the headlines again.

"Are you going to take me away, Bruce?"

As I became surprised, a familiar voice could be heard from behind me; I'd been snuck upon.

I turned to face the lady who had triumphed about creeping up on The Batman himself, and of course... of all citizens.

"You're quite distracted, aren't you?" she inquired. "Quite an accomplishment, Princess; I certainly didn't see you coming." I started quickly because I couldn't help but remember how lovely she appeared in her yellow sundress, revealing her gracious legs concealed under her flowing skirt.

She's as stunning as ever.

"The Batman uses Google; that's a different one," I say to her as I move into the computer where I was studying. Diana said it in a playful tone.

I totally missed what I was focusing on because I was completely overwhelmed.

I quickly switched off the monitor, leaving the black screen for her to gaze at. "It's nothing," I secretly whispered. She sent me a teasing smile, like she always does while we're together. When it comes to controlling my feelings, she's a scary princess. "Is that soooo..." Diana teased, "You haven't been answering my calls recently," she said quietly, "I've been distracted." I responded flatly, turning my focus back to the batting screen, which was still switched off, in the hopes of diverting my attention back to what I was doing earlier before she had the opportunity to interrupt me.

"Bruce..." she murmured.
When I heard her call my name, I turned to face her, something I obviously shouldn't have done.
Diana moved in closer to me when I saw her perfect cleavage peeking out from the opening of her shirt.

She's a jerk for being so careless.
I averted my gaze in the hopes of stopping the mesmerizing temptress who was attempting to entice me with her alluring bewitchment. She is so seductive that it should be illegal.
And I held my ground... for at least 5 seconds.
My eyes returned to hers when I watched her lips get closer to mine. Her warm breath lingered on my lips as she offered me a fearsome smile, the kind that lionesses send to their prey.
Now I'm the prey?
No, I'm smarter than this; I've faced much greater hazards and perils than what she's providing right now... still...
She rested her palms on my back and drew my head tighter to her.

She's special. When it comes to her, I feel almost helpless. Her enticing beauty is too powerful for my aching ego. I'm aware of the dangers of opening up and giving way to my impulses, but she's almost too irresistible to avoid at times.

She rubbed her palms across my cheeks as she drew my head closer and closer to her, eventually... yielding...

Tragic events occurred when a cock blocker in the shape of a hound came barking at my princess.

Ace, you have excellent timing.

I could've done something I'd deeply regret back then, but a part of me yearned to sample her luscious full lips or caress her lovely curves.

I couldn't decide if I was relieved or unhappy with the outcome.

Diana knelt in front of Ace because the dog was thrilled to see her. With an enthusiastic grin on his lips, he was rolling all over the house.

"For such a large dog, he sure has a soft spot for stunning Amazonians like you, huh?" I silence.

When I realized what I had just said, I felt a wave of embarrassment wash through me. It's not every day that I make mistakes like this.

My blunder most likely gave her the wrong impression about what I said. A blunder that would torment me for the remainder of the evening, a blunder that was costing her...

I just handed her...

I turned to face her, only to be met with the same teasing eyes she'd been showing me since earlier. I could sense the discomfort generated by her gaze.

"Did the Batman just thank me?"

Diana chuckled, her eyes tightening to a true leer.

"I-I-I-I-I-I-I-I-I-I-I-I-I-

"You think I'm a lovely Amazon princess?" "It's not what you hear!" she said. I respond frantically.

Diana broke out laughing as floods of joy welled up in her eyes. She was obviously becoming agitated every time I became agitated.

"Loud and simple, Bruce," she remarked sarcastically.

I stared down at the deck, defeated; the trails of weakness had replaced my desire to utter even the tiniest retort whilst the perpetrator herself was in front of me, grinning like a hyena.

She's been a little rough about her playfulness recently, which makes me question why...

It didn't take long for Diana to regain her composure when she switched to Ace, who was now on the ground rolling over. "Ace hasn't been feeding right lately?" she hummed to herself as she rubbed Ace's belly. "How the hell did you hear about that?" Diana inquired flatly.

Diana rolled her eyes, her lips curving into the corners of her cheek, "Duh, I saw that on your camera earlier," she sassed vehemently, "He's not ill, is he?"

With a worried expression on my face, I turned to face her.

"No, he isn't ill or something," I said.

I massaged Ace's back as I observed him asking for other affection; he is a really affectionate puppy.

"I guess I have an idea as to what makes him that way, Bruce," she said sternly.

My ears pricked up as my focus was drawn to Diana. She knows the solution to a question that not even Google knows about?

I turned to face her as I saw her take something from her small purse, which she had been wearing all along. My imagination got the better of me, and I caught myself looking at her like a kid at a zoo. "Here, Ace," Diana said, pulling out a slice of what seemed to be a carrot. She brought it up to Ace's nose, obviously leading him on when the hound leapt and grabbed it from her grasp.

What happened right now?

Ace, who hardly consumes something, was energized by only a slice of carrot that Diana carried.

"Diana, what was that?" "Amazon carrots, I brought some with me when I went back last week," I inquire, a touch of wonder in my voice. Diana uttered Amazon carrots, what makes "amazon carrots" distinct from all the meals we offer him every day. There must be a unique ingredient in it. "Amazon carrots, eh," he murmured.

"Are you curious, Bruce?" Diana teased claimed, "Do you like any as well?"

Darn, her advances tend to appear out of nowhere. I need to learn more about this so-called Amazonian carrot.

"No, I was just curious about how quickly you stimulated Ace's appetite," I said sternly, "I think Ace just likes me more than he likes you; he seems to consume more when I'm around." Diana sarcastically remarked that I had come up with a witty answer to her advances.

"Oh, maybe you should come by more frequently, princess, or maybe you should just stop here for sure," I say jokingly.

As I examined the bits of carrot Ace had left on the surface, my lips developed a confident smirk...

She's gone deafeningly still.

She might have made a witty retort at this stage.

She, on the other hand, did not.

I slowly twisted my head to face her, my hands clenched with nervousness. Why am I nervous all of a sudden? Damn it!

As I reflected on the terms, I had said to her earlier, a sudden wave of awareness washed through me.

She thinks I'm teasing, but she's not going to take it literally!

Just a minute... this is Diana we're worried about. Perhaps the most naive Princess in the world, if not the whole cosmos, if the Grail didn't work, but still...

I slowly turned to face her, only to see her looking at me with a blank expression, her gaze fixated on me for some purpose.

What is going on with her?

"You mean it?" her lips twitched as she bent in closer. Crap, she's doing it again, she uttered softly, her light eyes pulling me in. Now I'm too weak to do something or act rationally. When she's nearby, I'm trapped in my normal condition. I can see her lovely cleavage from this angle, which I had been denying, but my eyes kept betraying me.

I gaze into her eyes steadily, my mouth shivering; I can't even regulate my whole body anymore.

"Who are you, Bruce?" She inquired once more.

"Diana is a formalized paraphrase.

"Yeeeeeeeeeeeeeeeeeeeeeeeeeeeeeeeee " Diana hummed, her eyes gleaming with excitement.

I can't possibly suggest that was a prank, or she'll slap me to the bottom. I say I've experimented with many women's emotions before, but this one is nothing like the others. Ace can be seen sniffing the carrot bits in my lap as though he was hungry for what I was carrying.

So, there you have it. I may as well let her stay; the manor has been feeling lonely lately. I mustered all of my bravery to shape a sentence in my tongue: "Diana, Stay with..."

Alfred was the voice that distracted us from the communicator.

"Your supper has arrived, sire."

When I moved straight into the bat computer, I suddenly came to my senses.

"Be right there, Alfred," I said as I returned my heel to the princess, who was looking at me intently.

"Will you like to share supper with me, Diana?" I inquired in a persuasive tone.

She sprang to her feet, frantically brushing away a piece of hair that was waltzing in her direction.

For whatever excuse, seeing her like this makes me laugh; she's the way so much of a jerk at times. I approached her confidently, hands on her cheeks, other hand wiping off the loose strand to her left ear. I was too preoccupied with what I was doing to note her flushed face during it all.

"There, all is easier now," I murmured, "T-Thanks Batman, I mean Bruce..."

"In case you haven't learned earlier, have supper with me, Princess, and I'm not taking no for an answer," she said, making me laugh. I uttered with a sinister grin.

"Yeah, I'd love to," Diana responded excitedly. "Follow me, Princess," I uttered as I turned my heel towards the exit of the batcave when unexpectedly I noticed a warm grasp holding me back. Diana was the one." "Back then, it was race. What exactly were you going to suggest to me?" " She inquired, perplexed. "Today, we're getting Italian! Isn't that your favourite?"

I quickly changed the topic. The talk is cursed to ever be brought up.

"Anyway, let's go to the dining area, Diana," I said as I led her out of the bat cave. When walking next to her, I couldn't help but note her scowl.

I could sense the irresistible fragrance of the pasta hanging in the breeze as I approached the dinner table. "I know how this goes, Bruce," I said as I took out a chair for Diana. She expressed herself solemnly. Her glare was as frigid as the air outside.

She was obviously displeased with me for whatever reason. "Miss Diana, please do indulge tonight's supper that I cooked," Alfred said, coming from the kitchen. "I certainly would, Alfred; I won't let any jerk ruin this lovely evening for me." Diana retorted while staring daggers at my instructions.

Alfred saw and seemed concerned for a brief moment, giving me a puzzled expression. Regrettably, I'm almost as clueless as he is.

"Sire, I hope you enjoyed tonight's "Diana special." I spat out my drink as I shot the British butler a disapproving look; that was the last thing I expected Diana to hear tonight.
He didn't have to say something in front of the girls.

I gradually shifted my gaze to the princess, who was, sadly, enjoying the whole thing with her trademark mocking leer, which was based on me for some cause "Diana special, huh?" "The master is so organized to the extent that he also arranged a special meal for yours truly, miss Diana," Alfred said with a subtle chuckle. "hmm, that's odd, Alfred," I said, looking at her in a very ashamed way. "Got some other Bruce tidbits that I can know?" Diana joked.

"Oh, you're in for a treat, ma'am," Alfred answered as he drew out a chair.

Damn it, He completely revealed me to her. I'm at a loss for words when they all share my most shameful secrets.

Laughter hung in the air around the bleak and dark environment of the manor as I suddenly felt wet. All those days I dined alone in this large manor's dark mood were as gloomy as a sad bat hanging by a stuffy tree in solitude. It felt good and wet...

I lifted my head to see how content and joyful she was with Alfred.

When watching her from a distance, I can't help but smile.

"How does she just sit there and chuckle though looking so lovely?"

I was thinking to myself when she returned my attention with her trademark playful leer.

I locked my gaze on each other for a few seconds before looking down. When I looked under, I sensed a scratching feeling on my leg and found Ace sleeping on my foot.

I returned my attention to her, telling her a tale about her sister and how they cook food in Themyscira.

Now I understand why Ace was so at ease with her.

It isn't the carrot at all.

Her existence simply makes things easier. Her influence over others is so powerful that everything about her improves. It was her overall shine that illuminated all the darkest corners of the planet.

Her radiance eventually lifted the bleak tone of the Manor, which had always been sad and gloomy.

Maybe she'll be able to brighten my day then.

Maybe she'll be able to remain here permanently with me...

"Hey, Bruce, what's up with the silence over there?" Diana inquired almost out of nowhere.

It took me off balance because I was zoning out at the dinner table. "Nothing, I was just wondering how silly you sound when you chuckle," I joked. Diana said, "Nothing." "Oh, that's it; after this, you and I are going to have a one on one outside," I retorted sarcastically. She made a provocative challenge.

"Deal," I said, "do you think you can accommodate me?" Diana jokingly inquired

The discussion continued as the whole room burst out laughing.

If only the next few days were like this.

Soon, when I actually get up the nerve to question her...

"Diana" Project.

"Darn Him!"

I mutter to myself as I lie on my bed with the peachy feelings I've been harbouring since last week. It's been almost a month since I've seen him; it's as though he's left us or anything...

I was abandoned.

We did get into a scuffle the last time we talked. It has much to do with being so reckless on the front line and impacting the overall strategy.

If I understand it, he is the sort to pause and reflect before acting, but there is nothing wrong with confronting the danger head-on. He simply didn't trust me sufficiently to make my own choices and felt the need to always supervise me!

It's not that I despise it or anything. I think of it as him watching out for me, but he still goes crazy on the entire thing.

I did say some blunt words to him the last time we spoke, but in retrospect, I definitely shouldn't have said them to the guy himself. Later that evening, I recall digging my face deep into my pillows, my mind aching for me to apologise to him directly, but my stubbornness got the better of me.

And, considering my feelings for him, I agree that he should be the one to reach out to apologise, not me.

The person's circle of confidence is as thick as my ego, and that's saying a lot. Alfred is probably the only person who can break through his thick veil of caution.

But, as difficult as it is, him opening up to me is one of the things I've been praying to Hera for. Hera is aware of how many days I wanted to get him to open up to me, only to be pulled further even more.

I can't keep thinking of him all the time; I can't carry on like this. I need to live my life without The Dark Knight himself disturbing my thoughts.

So I exited my quarters and went to the cafeteria to create an Iced Mocha, making my mind calm. I waited for a moment until a woman's voice from behind me said, "How's the Blender Diana?"

Mari was dressed casually in a dress shirt and pyjama pants when I turned around. She had a crazy bed head, which I don't believe she realized. She most likely only awoke.

"I think it's still running," I answered casually.

She replied with a yawn and rubbed her eyes with her hands.

"Had a rough night?" "Yeah, it was a really rough night," I said. "Tree Planting? Ten hours of tree planting can exhaust everyone," she said. "I had no idea you were into that, Mari," I joked.

"It was for a fundraising fundraiser that John and I had organized," she said as she took a mug from the cupboard. He's been really interested in nature these days." "That's cool, Mari," Mari said. I took the blender and dumped the freshly blended mocha into my cup, followed by the ice cubes from the tiny tray.

"I can't wait until the next three months," Mari said dreamily, rubbing a diamond ring on her left ring finger, "Congratulations." Be sure to invite me, Mari," I said cheerfully, "Everyone in the league is welcome!" She said, "I'm glad for my dear friend, but I'm still envious." "So, how's the planning going?" Curious, I inquired.

Mari squeezed the powder from a pack of caffeinated coffee into her cup. "It's going well, Diana," she said after pouring hot water. I was initially concerned about the expense and financial requirements, but it seems that John has a very supportive supporter." Mari's response was delightful.

Hearing her comments reminded me of somebody in particular. The loneliness that I had for him is returning to torment me like a boomerang.

"Is that correct?" I gave a firm response.

"John assumes he's slick, but I know for a fact that Batman is going to pay for our wedding." Under the cold exterior, he's really a generous guy." "By the way, Batman hasn't been to the watchtower in a while. Have you learned anything about him?" Mari continued. "I know, you two are fairly together."

"I don't know, Mari, I don't know..." "Diana, is everything all right?" I asked. Mari inquired with worry. I saw her troubled face when she inquired. The last thing I want to do is irritate my friends regarding my condition. "Well, I'm good, Mari," I said with a nervous smile.

Mari glanced at me suspiciously as she sighed exasperatedly, "Isn't this about Batman?" "It's written all over your face, kid," Mari retorted.

"Are you sure I'm that open?" Mari shrugs it all off when she taps me on the back and asks, "Have you tried reaching out to him?" "Hmph, why should I?" she inquired. "It's not like we're together or something," I remarked. "If anything, he should be the one to reach out," I said. "I'm always joking about our last debate."

"Diana is indeed as obstinate as ever." "Follow your spirit, Diana, until it's too late," Mari replied.

Mari then walked away with her mug of coffee in hand after saying those terms. What exactly does she say by "too late?" I'm not sure what you're talking about.

Well, anyway.

I collected my thoughts and went to the workout room to let out some steam. When I arrived at my destination, I lost no time and headed straight to the punching bag field to distract myself from worrying about him. If he had been here, he might have already chastised me for not "stretching" before any physical exercise.

Yeah, he's bossy, but I know deep down that it's really his way of expressing love for me.

Why am I worried about him at all? I came here to divert my attention away from my mind wandering ever more casually through my imagination.

I worked on the punching bag, causing it to get much more creased than before.

I pound the punching bag with my aching fists, doing a perfect 1-2 combo with an elbow jab. I gave it a fast blow under when doing a grip that culminated in me pinning down the punching bag I had been abusing earlier.

This was the Punching Bag he had always used when he was working out or had free time. I can't help but grin as I recall how we used to spar here anytime he had spare time. He was still trying to get under my skin somehow, but checking an Amazon was the last thing he should've done to gain an advantage.

I recall him teaching me the 1-2 mix and how I sucked the first time. I spent nearly three hours perfecting it with him coaching me and fixing any error I created. He stood by me the whole time I worked my buttocks off to perfect the mix. He said something about "fundamentals," which lingered in the back of my mind for a while.

What exactly is fundamental?

I didn't even get a chance to ask him because he quickly corrected my shape after making a bad swing that didn't inspire him. I confess, I figured it was useless at first.

Since, first and foremost, I am a Meta and, secondly, I am Wonder Woman.

I was trained for fighting since birth, and I've always had warrior instincts. I saw myself as a mighty member who didn't require "fundamentals" because I was blessed with courage, grace, intellect, and elegance.

Despite my feeble requests, he remained firm in his conviction that each of us has a flaw that our adversaries can exploit one day. When facing off against enemies, one should always be uncertain, particularly when an intellectual genius like Luthor is present.

It came in handy once when Cheetah and I were fighting in Gorilla City. They had learned my battle patterns, and Cheetah had been practising all along. When I remembered the action that the Dark Knight had shown me, I felt humiliated because of how much of an advantage she had over me.

Cheetah came at me at a high tilt, anticipating a weak position on her waist. Cheetah seems to jump a lot as she's about to kick, but her waist is still free for any reversals. I took a step back and waited, watching her fiery smile intensify.

I felt amazing thinking my manoeuvre succeeded against someone who had reference to my battle patterns and had actually rehearsed it all only to be overcome by a new move as I evaded her claws, catching her waist from the side and threw her off a building which eventually shocked her.

She raised her eyes only to hiss at me as she struggled to free herself from my grip. I eventually knocked the cheetah out with a huge blow to her jaw.

I got up to see Batman, who had been studying me from a distance the whole time. He gave me a satisfied smile, which made me very happy on the inside. It seemed as though I'd accomplished something worthwhile. He offered me a respectful nod as he went on his way to look for casualties from Doomsday's rampage through the area, leaving me looking at him running gracefully. I just stood there with a proud expression on my forehead…

He was right all along; we can never feel too sure about ourselves because who knows what will happen the next day. Amid adversity, we can remain uncertain.

After that, we were recognized by the whole universe for once again saving the world. As we stood tall against the powers of darkness, we were showered with glory from all over the world.

He should have been there when we got the honorary recognition from the President of the United States himself. It was entirely due to his strategy that we were able to neutralize Doomsday and save more losses.

I realize he likes to operate behind closed doors, but... For all of his contributions in the league, a little praise or even a citation will suffice.

Hera, I always miss him...

I had always seen the positive in him when he first caught my attention, and I must confess...

He has always been the apple of my eye.....

What the hell am I worried about?

Hera, I came here to distract myself from The Dark Knight, just to become much more enamoured of him. I came to when I stood on my knees, resuming my training session with my Bat-punching bag.

This is pointless; I really can't keep him out of my mind. It's been like this for a couple of days now, and I'm beginning to miss him even more.

If he will just contact me right now...

Oh, how I longed for his deep baritone voice when my communicator unexpectedly got some kind of transmission.

"From Wonder Woman to Superman"

Ye, it's Kal.

I was hoping for something else, but I'm glad to hear "Yes, Superman?" from my pal.

"You're wanted at the Monitor Womb," he responded. But isn't today Batman's birthday?

I found myself sprinting into the monitor womb, my heart pounding as hard as my legs could carry me, ignoring anyone I passed by because I had just one guy on my mind.

I arrived at my destination after quickly fixing my hair and brows. I have to appear presentable in front of him.

"It's good to see you again!" I exclaimed when I stepped inside. "Bat..." I screamed.

The chair spins to show a scarlet speedster with his mouth full of nachos. "Hello, Wondy," he says. Flash welcomed him.

Ok, it wasn't who I was hoping.

"How are you, Flash?" I inquired, nodding my head from left to right in search of anyone "eh? So you found "him" because I'm here." Flash retorted jokingly.

He let out a small smile, which I didn't really like. I was so happy to see the guy again after all these years, only to be greeted by a scarlet jester who plays about too much, "Very Funny Flash, now where is he?" I inquired sternly.

Flash stared at me with a puzzled expression. He scratched his brow in befuddlement.

"Ummm, to what are you referring?" I rolled my eyes when I glanced at the television, only to find that a videogame had been stopped.

Wait a minute, Batman doesn't play video games...

What?

What really is going on?

"Batman, the man who was going to be assigned to oversee duties today. What happened to him?" When he got up from his chair, Flash's puzzled face became more apparent.

"Diana, who's Batman?" he demanded solemnly as I prepared to deliver a quick hit to the gut...

"All right, fine!" In ecstasy, I pronounced the word "flash." "He had stopped by earlier to have some updates on the monitor womb and the security breaches. He then suddenly quit. Anyway, now that you're here, will you take over my shift?" "He came by earlier?" " "And you didn't see the need to tell me of all people?" I finally demanded angrily.

"I mean, he did say he'd let me play NBA 2k20 if I didn't tell everyone he was heeeeeeeeeeeeeeeeeeeeeeeeeeeeeeeeeeeeeeeeeeeeeeeeeeeee "Oh damn!" gasped Flash.

I shot him a complete look and snapped my knuckles, hoping to slap the facts from the scarlet speedster who had inadvertently spilt some of the beans.

"What's going on, Wally?" "I want to hear!" I exclaimed.

"Yeah, I had something I needed to do back in Star Zone, so see you later, Wondy," he said as he dashed away like a train charging down a crowded expressway.

Something fishy is definitely going on here, Hera. I had my suspicions regarding his strange actions in recent days, but now I'm certain.

He's obviously ignoring me, and I'm curious why.

Now that my composure has worn thin, I'm going to get to the bottom of this, even though it means slamming a few senses into that dense skull of his.

With just one place in view, I dashed to the teleporter without delay.

Gotham City is a fictional city in the United States.

I've been waltzing through Gotham City Park for quite some time. I was scheduled to go to Wayne Manor to confront the man about his disappearance over the last few days, but I wanted to take a detour to clear my mind. I didn't have time to turn into anything else, so concealing my identity would be difficult, but luckily, there are just a few people here for the time being.

I hummed to myself as I scanned around for interesting things to see. I haven't had the time to go out in a long time, owing mostly to my overburdened missions. But right now, I'm having a good time in a park in Gotham.

His town. Bruce's town.

I slapped myself to get myself to stop daydreaming. I'm amid soul-searching. Thoughts of him have been bombarding my mind recently, and I want to be free of his grip over me.

I looked at the marvellous statue that stood in the middle of the park, the ice cream shop, and the lake with large swans swimming, which I believe acts as some sort of vehicle or float with the lovely garden behind it, which will be a perfect tourist spot for couples. I couldn't help but be mesmerized when seeing a couple on a boat trip just enjoying themselves. They were clutching each other, with the lady resting her head on the man's back. Suddenly, I pictured myself and a certain someone in the same circumstance in this wonderful position, with passion in the breeze as we float together with the intimate mood hovering in the air.

It's getting late, and I didn't even realize I was in this situation until I find myself sitting on my hands with a silly grin on my face.

Diana, are you serious? This is the second time today for the 16th time this week.

Why can't I keep him out of my head?

I've been daydreaming about him for weeks now, and it seems like there's nothing I can do to keep him out of my mind.

His hold over me is too intense for even a strong Amazon warrior like me to tackle.

It's too much for me.

I wanted to see him right away!

I soared across the park, unafraid, towards a destination that I had set my sights on. As I walked by, I could hear people cheering, "Look, it's Wonder Woman!!"

"Lady Wonder!! "What is she doing in Gotham?" "I'm a huge fan." "

I wasn't paying attention to them at the time. I'm so preoccupied with something or someone that I just need to see and chat, and

I'm not going to take no for an answer. If I have to pound some sense into his dense head just to get him to open up to me, I'll happily do it.

As I continued on my way, I could sense the freezing breeze blowing across my skin. It's getting me nervous for some reason. Is it really essential for me to be here?

As I drove towards my goal, I ignored the thoughts forming in the back of my mind.

As I rang the doorbell, I realized I had arrived at my destination. I rubbed my hands together in anticipation, pacing back and forth like a toy train on a revolving rail. I note that there are several people in the area around the manor.

There seemed to be a group going on right now.

I was so rushed from inside that I didn't even have time to transform into a more comfortable dress. I let myself in and flew through the gates to the garden where the people were congregating.

I didn't give a damn anymore. I can't keep my anger in check any longer. I wanted to get my feelings through to him in every way I could.

All those sleepless nights wondering how he's going, what he's eaten, whether he's doing good, and who he's with?

What he's up to...

No, no.

As I mumbled those severe sentences, a thought occurred to me.

I slipped behind the bushes while I took another peek around the manor, spotting Batman without his bat armour. He was dressed beautifully in a well-tailored suit, with a neatly folded blue handkerchief in his suit pocket.

After all those days of dreaming about him, I actually saw him. When I was about to approach him, I felt a warmth brew inside me as I saw something.

He conversed with others, a lady with fair hair wearing a sweet red dress and carrying what seems to be a bottle in her left side.

"I'm curious who he's with..." I recall the feelings I had earlier when my hands stiffened and formed fists. I suddenly felt hostile for no apparent cause.

Then I felt depressed as I saw Bruce so pleased with the lady he was happily talking to.

He may be now found someone with whom he can connect and trust.

Is this what Mari was referring to earlier when she said those terms to me?

That's also why he's been so quiet about the league lately; he's probably planning on getting married and leaving the league...

As the idea of him being with someone else lingered in my head, I felt my heartache. The thought of him being with someone other than me is too much for me to bear.

I couldn't bear the thought of him slipping away from me, no matter how tough I am. I can't bear the thought of him slipping into someone else's arms instead of mine. I can't stand it when he chooses someone else over me...

Why am I acting this way...

As strange as it might be, He is the explanation why my life has been filled with rainbows and sunlight. It was him who taught me how beautiful life is outside of Themyscira ever since I appeared in Man's world. It was him who taught me to never give up despite the odds being stacked against me, to always be prepared for something, to always strive to be better every day and to have confidence in my teammates to surpass all expectations I might have imagined.

He forced me to do something I could never have considered doing before. It was he who opened the way for my aspirations to come true that I could not have seen in my wildest dreams.

That's how much of an influence he's had over me, and I'll never consider losing him to anyone else.

No, it does not...

When a drop slowly falls to the ground, tears begin to form in my eyes and run down my cheeks to my chin. I gently caress the moisture on my face, perplexed.

I'm sobbing.

Excruciating flashes of him with someone else hang in my mind once more. The agony in my abdomen is too much for me to bear.

I'm not supposed to be here.

I buried my face in my hands and turned on my heel to go anywhere, somewhere that wasn't here.

I wasn't paying attention to my surroundings when I happened to run into someone. I dropped to the ground in a rather precarious state for whatever cause. As a warrior in this pathetic state, I looked up to apologise to the individual I'd come across, only to see a silhouette of someone recognizable in the brilliant moonlight. Someone gave me a hand to support me get up. I welcomed his help as I covered my face in my hands to wipe the tears that were now streaming from my eyes.

"Princess..." says the narrator.

I was only brushing away my tears when I noticed a dark and baritone voice. My heart was racing so hard that I lifted my head to see My Dark Knight himself standing in front of me, his handsome yet brooding profile. The sensation and emotion that had been aching to break out inside me have resurfaced. I tried to keep my feelings in check as I stood firm on my feet, bitter in my core.

"What exactly are you doing here?" I evidently inquired when sniffling. "Shouldn't you be hosting your friends over there?"

"I guess that's going to be my side," he said sternly, "what are you doing here?" I didn't know what to say. I couldn't tell him the truth about why I came to see him and how much I had missed him in recent weeks. I was speechless when I stared back at him, "y-your bride..." I said quietly.

Bruce appeared perplexed as he heard my words. He laughed quite a little as he stared at my pitiful condition.

"I think you have the wrong idea about this whole thing, Princess," he admitted, "but I do intend on dancing with the gorgeous lady tonight." I stared daggers at him as he gave me his trademark arrogant smirk.

He suddenly recalled something: "Crap, I can't be seen with Wonder Lady; it'll definitely lift their suspicions."

He cast a glance behind me at someone or something. I turned around to see Alfred, who responded with a smile. The butler approached the visitors, who were comfortably chatting on the grass.

"Can I please have everyone's attention?" Amid the crowd, Alfred cried out, "Ladies and gentlemen, please. Today's Let us gather in the main hall; the party is about to begin."

Everyone then went in, much as the British butler had instructed. He was about to walk in when he turned to Bruce with a smile and closed the door.

I saw my arm shift as though a force was attempting to take it away from me; I turned around to find him pulling my arm somewhere.

"Come along with me, Princess."

His voice was dark and stern, but for some reason, after hearing his mysterious timbre for so long, I felt wet.

My feet were floating on their own, and my lips were curving into a wide grin. I was meant to be withdrawn from my feelings for him, but I couldn't help but be excited about what was going on. We haven't had much alone time in a long time.

We came to an abrupt halt for some explanation. "Are you okay?" He inquired, concerned, "Oh, I'm perfectly well, Bruce," to which I replied with a smile.

He glanced at me for a couple of seconds before raising a fake grass bushel that was too natural to be seen. Underneath, there was some kind of gap that would lead to... "The Batcave?" I think if I had to guess again. Curious, I inquired.

Bruce sent me a little grin and a few glances.

"You're turning into a detective yourself, princess." He said enthusiastically, "Thanks, I learned from the highest." I teasingly replied, but he didn't seem to care. He opened the slid door while he smiled at me as though he wanted me to hop in.

"Can you tell me what's going on?" I inquired, a little nervously.

He lifted his head as he maintained the same expression against me " "Oh! "I'm not going in," I yelled angrily, "but you are." " He replied in a light tone, "I said n..."

I saw more people come in from the entrance as they were about to reach the Wayne Manor as I mumbled the terms. We were almost seen when Bruce unexpectedly yanked my hand away from him and dashed straight to the opening, covering the lid with the bush on top as before.

We were actually sinking lower and deeper into the earth, with darkness surrounding me. That I could see was illumination at the very top. I screamed with delight as I saw gravity drag me to the ground.

"This I sssssssssssssssssssssssssssssssssssssssss I screamed angrily at the top of my lungs.

"I'm sorry," I remorsefully said, wailing my palms back and forth before I inadvertently struck him in the chest. "Just hold it together and calm down, Princess," he replied gently.

It was too dim to see him, but I could hear his monotone voice from behind me. "I turned my head from left to right, still in shambles, when I felt a force locking each of my shoulders in place.." "princess, princess, princess, Don't worry. Simply shut your eyes and listen to my speech. We'll be there soon. "When I heard his monotonous voice again, I felt warm. I closed my eyes and pictured him hugging me back...

"Take a deep breath!"

"What?" I exclaimed. "Just do it!"

Make a splash!!

All inside me became sticky all of a sudden. As I opened my eyes, I realized I was underwater.

Is it possible that we're in the centre of the sea?

As he pulled me tightly and we submerged to the surface, I saw a silhouette of him approaching from above.

I took a deep breath and looked around; this location seems to be familiar. From above, bats were buzzing about. The fragrance of dunes and the echo of a waterfall cascading...

Is this the Batcave?

"You could've only drifted in midair, you know, but in any case, use this," I said as I turned around to see Bruce drenched. He was handing me a towel, to which I said, "Thank you." "Join me," he said sternly, and I rose to my feet, following the man himself. "Is this the Batcave?" I asked hastily, moving my feet quickly next to him. "I inquired." "Yeah, the innermost portion of it," Bruce said. "Tim found the tube." "Like?" I created a hidden entrance in case anything urgent happened." " I inquired, "Like what happened earlier?" He replied sternly, which piqued my interest; as predicted, Batman is always prepared for something. Then all of a sudden, he came to a halt.

"So, what brought you here?" He questioned seriously, and I could hear the urgency in his voice, "I uhhhh..." I murmur to myself.

I came up with a few reasons to use. There was no chance in Hera's name I was going to inform him, "I just came here to see you", and get us in a lot of trouble. "I came here to report about uh," I nervously uttered, "Flash's blunder."
"Mistake?" He inquired, and I attempted to maintain a straight face to save him from detecting my flimsy deception. He has a keen sense of others.

"You are such a lousy thief, princess," Bruce says as he shuts his eyes. "Since then until now," he joked. "There's really no fooling the world's best investigator in the world."

"What did you want the group to be for?" "I uh..." I mumble softly, "I figured it was your wedding reception."

Bruce gave me a disgusted look and chuckled in answer to my query, "Are you for real?" He questioned teasingly, pausing to collect himself.

"Well, Batman, you should laugh all you want, but I'll get you for this eventually." "the race, It's not even amusing," I joked. "By the way, I really haven't forgotten about our last disagreement, you know."

His grin vanished, replaced by what seemed to be a concerned look on his forehead. "I'm sorry for speaking those words to you, Princess," he pled honestly, and I was perplexed at what had just happened. I can see in his eyes the utmost honesty as if he really believed every word of it. I really shouldn't have brought it up. "For what?" I inquired. "Our most recent talk wasn't really good." He reported that "I might have gone crazy with my dominance over you," I recall thinking after our argument over him being overprotective and watchful over me.

"You're correct; I've been really careful around you, not offering you the confidence you needed," he said.

His attention remained fixed on the ground the whole time, and his speech was tinged with regret and sorrow. "Is it why you didn't even come to see me at all?" I could tell he was upset about our disagreement. Curious, I inquired.

He lifted his head to meet my gaze but then averted his gaze.

"I tried to, but..." "Duty calls," he said calmly.

"What do you mean, duty?" I inquired.

What exactly does he mean by duty?

"Well, one of my business associates, Lucius Fox, is celebrating his 30th wedding anniversary with his wife today at the Manor," he said.

I had a suspicion there was more to "Lucius Fox" than meets the eye.

"Just a corporate associate? How did he convince you to consent to get the group here?"

"I informed him if he didn't, I'd beat his a$$ for sure."

A sound from elsewhere in the cave echoed across the cave. As I turned around, I saw an elderly man in a waistcoat seated in the chair in front of the bat computer.

Bruce approached him and tapped him on the back. They seem to be really acquainted with one another.

"What's going on?" "Meet Lucius Fox, Diana. The mastermind behind it all, "Bruce said confidently

What's the matter, Lucius? Who was the guy he was referring to?

What is he doing in the Batcave?

What really is going on?

"I'm sorry, I'm confused," I admitted, "but it's good to meet you, Mr Fox."

"Likewise, Miss Diana," Lucius said, "let's only assume that I am the one in charge of all the technologies here." I was taken aback for a second, but I now completely understood. Wait, does the fact that he's here say...

"Does that say you're conscious that..."

"Yes, Miss Diana, I knew Batman before he was Batman," Lucius said.

"So, how's our update going, Lucius?" Bruce asked, clearing his throat.

"Smooth as sugar, Mr Wayne," Lucius replied. "I already installed the firmware under which the data from the previous overhaul was applied to the last version." "It's safe to assume the Diana project is now over." He spurted uniformly.

Is that my name I just heard?

Lucius realized his error when he looked at Bruce with an uneasy smile on his lips, "I'm sorry," he said quietly, "Darn you, Fox." Bruce reacted.

They were speaking in hushed tones, but I could still hear them. What exactly is the Diana project?

Alfred's speech spoke out of nowhere from the bat speakers. computer's

"Mr Fox, you're wanted in the lobby," Alfred explained. "That's it for my cue. It was a pleasure to meet you, Miss Diana." Lucius reported before actually departing.

Though Bruce remained quiet, I observed him walk towards the exit. "Bruce?" I inquired, the Diana project already working in the back of my mind.

"Diana..:" he says quietly, turning back to face me. "This was going to be a treat, but now that you're here."

He clicks a key on the screen, and a large symbol appears in the bat-computer. It was named "The Diana Project" and said, "This is the Diana Project." When Bruce saw the screen, he said, "I was just confused." I was plagued with a slew of concerns.

"Whoa... whoa... whoa... whoa... whoa... whoa... whoa... whoa... "I inquired." "Everything you need to talk about becoming a competent Justice League participant is compiled in this book. Anything from combat techniques to mental conditioning is covered. I also installed the most recent addition, the thesis regarding the Legion of Doom and all of our other potential enemies in the future, "he replied

He pressed a bell, revealing all members of the Legion of Doom, along with their strengths and weaknesses.

"Each of the members you see there has their own set of strengths and weaknesses. After analyzing the numbers, you'll have an edge the next time, and you'll recognize how they'll behave or how you can fight whatever advances they produce." He also added, "I've already created a few recommendations about how the area of resources might learn from their flaws.

As I turned to face him, I was astounded by all he had taught me in the bat-computer.

"Did you do all of this for me?" I inquired.

Bruce averted his gaze as though he was attempting to keep everything inside of him bottled up.

"Ok, well," he said, "that's why I've been so distant from the league lately, but I'll have you know that this final product will be used as a final feedback on the next update that I did earlier."

"You didn't even call to let me know you were coming by earlier..." I muttered to myself, "I suddenly felt my heart becoming heavy for some excuse." Everything about what he said left me uncomfortable.

I finally summoned the nerve to challenge him once and for all.

"How did you come up with this, Bruce?" "What's the purpose of this "mission," I demanded sternly.

"I'll have you noted that the changes are going to kick in tomo..." he grinned as he turned his back to me and typed something on the screen.

I didn't let him finish until turning him around to face me head-on, saying, "Look at me, Bruce." "Why are you doing this?" I yelled angrily.

His eyes were shaky as he attempted to find elsewhere else than my eyes. His lips were shivering, and he attempted to talk, but none came out. "I could see he was in as much pain as I am." "....concluded that I was mistaken. You didn't need any assistance. You're this Amazon Fighter who embodied everything that a true heroine and warrior could be. Grace, intelligence, power, dedication, and..." He said it hesitantly.

When I heard his words, I could sense his sincerity; he was still having difficulty expressing himself, but I could tell he was trying his utmost.

"I've worked hard all this time to make you a stronger fighter and hero. I've done whatever I could to help you become a stronger version of yourself."

He said sternly, " "But there's nothing I can do to support you any longer; my lessons are most likely keeping you down from reaching your full potential, and I can't bear that. However, through this initiative, you will be able to improve and develop on your own. Without someone keeping an eye on you and..."

He took a brief break. I'm really speechless for the time being. I had no idea he felt this way about me...

"Without me stifling you. With this, you won't need me around as much "With a hurtful grin, he said

When I slapped him hard, I felt my feelings surge into my palms. "Stupid," I said, as tears streamed down my cheeks and my heart raced quicker than normal. "How ignorant can you be, Bruce?" I yelled angrily.

He was taken aback as he saw my outburst. He wasn't anticipating this kind of reaction from me.

"I came to see you because I missed you! I yearned for you!
I couldn't keep you out of my head during your absence. I couldn't sleep because you were everything I could think about!" I screamed violently.

Bruce was taken aback as he saw my outburst.

"W-What exactly do you mean? ...."

"I'm head over heels in love with you, Bruce Wayne!" I burst out laughing.

I didn't keep anything secret. He needs to realize how I feel about him and how deeply he has penetrated my mind and heart in every way. I'll confess it now.

He took a step back, a puzzled look on his lips.

"What are you talking about? Why should I?" He inquired, " "I'm not sure! Bruce, I can't help myself. "In answer, I yelled.

He took one more step further.

"There are loads of other guys out there that are great than me!" he exclaimed, "you should do better than falling in love with a mess like me!"

"You're the one I'm looking for, Bruce..." "I said softly. "Don't you get it? I adore you."

When I saw him attempting to flee, I took a little closer to him. I instinctively grabbed his arm to keep him from moving.

"Diana," he murmured, "don't run away from me, Bruce." "I can't take another day without you beside me anymore," I whispered, heartbroken.

"NO!" he exclaimed.

He attempted to get rid of me by fighting my grip, but it didn't succeed.

"Let... go!" he yelled loudly, "Talk to me!" "You don't get; We can never be together!" I conceded, to which he replied, "WHY?" I inquired vehemently.

He lowered his head and turned to face the deck.

I slowly raised his head to see his eyes, which were filled with despair and sadness, when all of a sudden...

"Diana, I'm... You have captured my attention. Your very existence is enough to make me tense; I love how you're so compassionate and honest to everyone; I love how naive and even immature you are. I admire your intelligence and your willingness to express yourself to others. I admire how, considering your dominance, you have a soft spot for people like me..."

"Brother Bruce..." I muttered under my voice, "I can't believe it..."

"And it isn't even the half of it..."
"I am captivated by your lovely expression, your streaming raven locks, your seductive gaze, your curves, and...."

He paused for a moment before saying, "Your lips" "Lips that I have been dreaming of kissing, fantasies that have often left me helpless because whatever I do..... You'll never be mine."

He went for my face but stopped in the centre.

I could sense tears welling up in my eyes once more.

"You're way too beautiful for me, Princess." He said it with an evil grin. "You are entitled to more."

"Why are you still inflicting pain on yourself to appease those around you?" I inquired vehemently, "Bruce, you're nice enough for me. Please give us a shot. Please allow me to be a part of your life. And tell me what troubling you are!"

He reached for my face, wiping out the tear that was falling down my cheeks. As he kissed me, he tucked a loose strand of hair behind my ear.

"Please forgive me for causing you concern, princess, just one day. I'll be brave enough to admit you." He spoke quietly.

I feel at ease, and the energy I felt as he whispered in my ears put me at ease. Despite our damp clothing, his body heat was enough to keep me warm.

My feelings, which I'd been struggling to keep hidden, have now hit him. Here I am, surrounded by the guy I deeply adore. Hello, Hera. "Bruce," I said, "if this is a dream, please never wake me up." He said, "Do me a favour" "What is it?"

"Please exclude the project from the list. There will never be a day when I will not need your presence. Stay with me. I want you to be there with me if it's as supervision or anything else. Forever and ever…"

From where I was, I could hear his slight chuckle. It made me feel relieved. "As you wish, Princess," he replied honestly.

Bruce slowly pulls forward, looking me in the eyes. His rich brown eyes are so mysterious and captivating that I might look at them for hours.

"Let's get out of these boots, Princess," he gently said.

My muscles were trembling at the time. I'm not sure I'm happy yet, but I've always been prepared for this...

"Yes, Bruce, please take me," I replied with a solemn expression on my forehead.

Bruce became surprised and agitated about what I had just said, saying, "N-NO..... That's not what I intended." He said tensely.

Oh, well. I was pleased but saddened at the same moment. How exactly does it work?

"However, just take a shower first, and ill plan the dress you'll be carrying," he begged.

What are you talking about?

"Dress...?" "Yes, Diana?" I inquired. Bruce said bravely. "Be my date and join me for a party." Dance?

"Are you with him?" "Still, I assumed you didn't want to be photographed with me. Everyone would be suspicious." I said, "Well, I do like to take chances from time to time..." " He reasoned, "Also..." he added

With the most charming grin I've ever seen him do, he stared at me with eyes so mysterious and dark that it practically made my heart flutter on the spot. "I want to dance with the most stunning lady tonight," he said.

Night at the Movies

"Hera, Bruce, this is absolutely fantastic!"

Diana screamed in joy as she licked an ice cream cone with her left side. It was her first time trying a delicacy like this.

Bruce was right behind her, with what seemed to be an ice cream cone in his right hand. They had just ended a task in Gotham City Park fighting off Bane and Giganta, which turned out to be very easy.

Perhaps because the powerful Amazon Princess had been battling alongside him the whole time, all he wanted to do was pull down Bane's venom tubes, and Giganta was well taken care of by the lady beside him, eating ice cream like a little girl "Bruce, you must tell me how they render this so tasty." Diana spat out a bit of cream on her nose.

Batman smiled softly as he reached into his tool belt for a handkerchief.

"Princess, you remember how you can be very immature at times?" He uttered as he handed her the handkerchief.

Diana made a huge pout at him, making her cheeks appear puffy and big. "A Handkerchief?" she asked, turning to the handkerchief he was holding out to her. She inquired as she licked the top of her ice cream cone.

"Hey, you were too preoccupied with the ice cream to note the huge bubble of cream on your nose." He snidely remarked

She immediately took the handkerchief from Bruce's grasp to clean away the cream, but as she was about to dab it on her nose...

She devised a genius idea, and a villainous grin appeared on her mouth. "I'm sorry, I didn't have my mirror with me, Bruce," she gushed, trying to catch his eye.

Bruce then took the bait and turned to face her with a vacant look, "It's basically all on you, no..."

"I don't know where it is, Bruce!" she exclaimed dramatically.

Bruce sighed and removed the handkerchief from her grasp to do it himself.

"The league's most professional warrior incapable of scratching her nose," he remarked sarcastically.

When he returned his attention to Diana, he found that she was sitting over with her eyes closed. As he read about her condition, he became instantly agitated. Diana wants more than a simple rub on her nose as she says, "What's the matter, Bruce? Hurry up." Diana said it in a lighthearted tone.

Her eyes were still closed, but a grin was steadily forming on her lips. Bruce's attention was drawn to her luscious lips, which she is keeping exposed and unguarded.

"She's so reckless, damn it," Bruce thought to himself, keeping his feelings at bay.

Bruce's phone abruptly emitted a sharp beep. Martian Manhunter was the name. Bruce picked it up right away to answer the phone.

Diana opened her eyes, dissatisfied with how things had turned out once again. The guy keeps being rescued by the ring, and it's getting rusty. This was not the first time unforeseen events had completely disrupted them.

"Yes, we're coming," Bruce said as he turned off the communicator.

He returned his gaze to Diana, who was wearing a depressed expression on her lips. She was delicately caressing her cone, her gaze fixed on the milk.

"Are you okay?" Batman told her genuinely.

Diana regained consciousness after recognizing Batman's speech. She must have been distracted by something to be taken off balance like that.

"Yeah, I'm fine Bruce, I mean Batman," he says. She responded hesitantly.

Batman moved in deeper to check on his mate. He may be a vile frozen teammate, but seeing Diana in despair is the last thing he needs to do.

"Princess," Batman said quietly. "Do you have anything on your mind right now?"

Diana turned to face him, remembering how near they are. It was unusual for Batman to be so worried about her, so she wanted to play a little prank on his overprotective knight.

"You want to be very concerned about me, Batman; maybe you're actually warming up to me?" Diana made a playful remark.

"You seem to be fine about how casual you are about your frail teasing. We are needed to return to the Watchtower, "Batman replies when turning away from her.

Diana responded with a sigh and a roll of the eyes. He was too naive to pick up on the clues she was dropping. Bruce is a master of the game of hard to get.

Regardless of how much space he focuses on between the two of them, Diana's unwavering hope and resolve to be with the guy she loves is stronger than everything else. She just stood there, smiling to herself, watching Batman step into the unseen plane.

"Are you coming?" He screamed from afar, "Oh, I'm certainly coming for you, my brooding warrior," she said softly to herself, "Yeaahhhh, be right there." Diana was convinced that she and Bruce might mean anything if he would only give them a shot. Shortening the gap between them would be a major obstacle that she can embrace to get closer with each move she makes. The possibility of getting him in her life is a significant gamble she can face.

"And with that, the conference is adjourned."

Since J'onn declared that the lengthy conference had come to an end, everyone scattered from the meeting board.

Before leaving, the representatives suddenly conversed with one another. Clark was checking in on Diana about the task when John was casually talking with Shayera. Flash, on the other side, remained seated, taking his time to calm his back.

"Finally, it felt like I was back in school again, listening to a long, dull lecture or something," Flash said, stretching his back.

"Pardon me for being dull, Flash." In answer, J'onn said, " "J'onn, it's not your fault. Unfortunately, whatever you were debating did not pique my curiosity." "Maybe you should bring some more time into paying care, Wally," Flash insisted. Diana said as she joined in on their chat, "This material is critical for all league members, you know." "Wow, I've heard it all before, Wondy. The same alerts and news as in previous missions" "I bet if it were about the latest cheeseburger varieties or how the Los Angeles Lakers dominated the recent NBA Playoffs, you'd be head over heels in listening to it," Flash replied. John spoke brusquely.

"Of course, Anthony Davis and LeBron James deserved the chip," Flash replied attentively, confirming John correct. "Man, you're as predictable as the Sun rising in the east," John joked, laughing loudly.

Shayera then walks over to them, carrying what seems to be a cup of coffee in her left hand.

"I don't question John in the least." "Hey, what's that going to mean?" Shayera interjected. "I guess what John said was you are proving his argument by being a bit too busy, Wally," Flash replied, obviously annoyed by what John and Shayera had said. "Wow, come on, ya'll are actually going to team up on me like this?" Clark said as he joined the discussion. Wally replied

The founding members' laughter and ambient conversation flooded the conference space. Diana was getting the time of her life, having the time of her life interacting with her peers like this without a care in the world.

She then sees something out of the corner of her eye. On his way out of the conference room, a caped crusader seemed to be in a rush to enter or at least listen to their fascinating chatter.

Diana decided to pursue Batman down the corridor. She ignored the gang's banter and proceeded to the gate, where she had last seen the caped crusader.

It didn't take long for them to remember Diana walking away quietly, without even saying goodbye. They just had one thought as they stared at each other.

"So, who's up for a pizza?" Flash eventually broke the silence by asking.

Bruce was tired and anxious, and what he needed was a decent night's sleep. He was heading down the corridor, past other participants who were comfortable speaking with each other.

Nothing will discourage him from running straight for the teleporter and a nice night's rest at the manor. He yawned to himself until he was interrupted by a voice from behind him, "Going somewhere?"

He turned around suddenly, annoyed by this guy behind him, to cast this irritating lecher off, only to find Diana welcoming him beautifully with her normal gleaming bright sapphire eyes.

"Oh, it's just you, Diana," he said glumly. He was too exhausted to even offer him a half-smile.

Diana cocked her head in reaction to his response. His passive sound irritated her.

"What do you think I'm the only one?" Diana grumbled in a resentful sound.

Batman couldn't help but yawn as he rubbed his neck in reaction to her nag. "Look, what do you like, Diana?" he thinks to himself. "I'm too tired after today's entire mess," Batman said flatly.

Diana leers at her, her fists making what seemed to be a hunch.

"You said earlier today that we'd watch a movie after the mission." She screamed violently, and Batman's mouth fell when he realized what he had done. He had utterly forgotten about his "promise" to her.

"Can we switch this to another day, Diana?" "I'm too tired to even last an hour," Batman insisted.

Diana's lips developed an evil grin after seeing his answer. The Amazon River Princess devised a nefarious scheme for the guy himself.

"Oh, you mean The Dark Knight of Gotham, the most feared caped crusader of the Justice League, is going to backtrack on his promise only because he's tired?"

Diana said intriguingly, attempting to taunt the man himself.

"Princess, what are you getting at?" Batman's eyes widened in reaction to Diana's outburst. He inquired menacingly.

Diana turned back, facing the other direction, while the incomprehensible guy remained obstinate. "Oh well, I think that's just who you are, Batman," she said. Diana spurted as she walked in the same direction. "Next time, don't give commitments you can't keep."

She was doing everything she could to provoke him and make him feel bad.

She took two moves in the opposite direction, awaiting his answer...

When all of a sudden, "Wait!"

Diana closed her eyes, ecstatic that her scheme had succeeded. "Yes?" she had Batman just where she needed him all along. "It's just for an hour....right?" Diana said, a little sad-faced. Bruce inquired cautiously.

The Amazon turned back to face his Dark Knight's wretched guilty look. "It's okay, Bruce," she quietly murmured, "I don't want to get in the way of your "brooding" alone time. "It's nothing like that!" she wanted to bring more heat to the flames to ensure he would never go back on his promise. Batman shouted out, attempting to clear up the confusion. "I'm far so exhausted from today's mission," Bruce says. "I understand," Diana said with a wicked grin she realized Batman couldn't bear. "I'm only going to see it all myself, even if a certain Caped Crusader promised to see it with me." Her acting talents are certainly on point right now. She could see it was making an impression on him.

"Anyway, Bruce, have a nice rest," Diana said angrily as she turned away.

Batman chuckled to himself, thinking she'd go to some length to make him feel worse. He responded with a smile, deciding to support Diana's efforts.

"OK, Princess, where should we watch this film?" Diana then offered Batman a mocking smile, leaving Batman ever more nervous.

"Ok, the film room is still under maintenance, so we'll have to catch it in my bedroom," Diana suggested.

"Do you live in your apartment?" Batman screamed a little.

He could see for himself that this was a terrible spot for the two of them to be apart.

"We won't be able to see the movie there, Dia..."

"Oh, then you're going back on your word now?" Diana cut in with a fierce expression in her eyes.

Batman sighed once more; her advancements appear to come out of nowhere.

"Let's go through this with Princess." Batman irritably replied.

Diana couldn't help but laugh, understanding how skilled she is at manipulating the scenario. When he abruptly turned to face her, she changed her posture.

"All right, let's get started," Diana said with a pleased smile.

Bruce found himself sitting next to the Amazon Princess again, watching a video, this time in her bedroom. She was too preoccupied with the movie to catch him peering at her from the corner of his eye.

The whole setup of the space seemed too good to be real. There were candle lights in the space, romantic background music (True - Spandau Ballet), and soft lighting.

"She sure did good with this arrangement," he thinks to himself as he returns his focus to the film.

Diana turned to look at his handsome warrior, who this time didn't have his helm shielding his ears. She smiled to herself when she searched for a pocketbook under her bed titled "How to Make This Night Romantic." She bent in quietly to her left to get a closer peek at the book's contents.

Bruce was too preoccupied with the film to remember Diana reading the pocketbook from her left hand. She made an effort to keep this as hidden from him as possible, trusting that this night would end happily.

Bruce yawns casually when he sees Diana, who isn't paying attention to the movie that they were meant to see together. He didn't need to glance at the book cover to find out what was in the pocketbook. His lips curl into a wide grin as he watches her work so hard to make this "movie night" great.

He returned his focus to the movie and saw the scene made him feel uncomfortable suddenly. The two actors in the film were now really similar to each other, just centimetres apart from touching noses.

And it did happen.

In the film, the two of them shared a hot and romantic kiss. The protagonists savoured each other's flavours as their hands roved all over their bodies. Their lips collided, escalating into a full-fledged gladiatorial brawl, and Bruce was there to see it.

He cast a quick look at Diana to see how she was reacting to anything, but she was already busy with her little pocketbook, to his dismay.

For a brief moment, Bruce felt at ease, but he was still concerned about how she might respond if she saw what was going on in the movie. After watching them strip off their clothes and begin to taste each other, Bruce went into panic mode, praying for the whole sequence to stop instantly.

"Please, please, please, please, please, please, please, please, please, please, "It would be too uncomfortable for me and Diana to watch this, particularly with the two of us alone.... in her quarters," Bruce reasoned.

As their voices got louder and louder by the second, a bead of sweat formed on his right eye. She would have noticed their passionate voices echoing from the movie if it hadn't been for the background music.

Diana was surprised when the girl's voice let out a loud moan, and she returned her focus to the movie. As she saw what the actors were doing, her mouth fell. They were so close to each other that she wondered if they were even acting.

Her focus was drawn to Bruce, who was wearing a very uneasy smile on his forehead. He was not loving the intercourse that was taking place in the film. Bruce returned her attention as he sensed a surprising desire rise from inside him. His gaze was drawn to her full, luscious lips, which were too tempting to ignore—those lips he had wished to kiss earlier.

Bruce's tongue pressed against the roof of his sealed mouth, eager to savour her wonderful lips and keep her tight. He could sense the intimacy lingering in the breeze, cutting like a knife.

Diana was looking straight at him, her heart beating furiously as if every beat was a go-ahead warning to pound him right here and call him hers. She could tell from the way he looked at her that he felt the same way. Diana's body is filled with a burning desire as she stares at his mysterious dark brown eyes, which seem to have finally captivated her.

"Bruce..." Diana bent in tight, her mind jumbled by the flood of feelings obstructing her ability to think clearly. She desired that more than anything else.

She needed Bruce to be just where she wanted him to be.
She could tell he was tense because his lips were shivering for whatever reason this time.
Diana kept leaning in closer, eventually closing the gap between them. Her nose was tickled by his warm breath, which left her nervous.
Diana is just a few inches removed from realizing her long-held ambition. She's had a lot of sleepless nights, and she's been dreaming about him and only him. Those romantic fantasies of them being together that she's had have made her even more head-over-heels in love with the Dark Knight.
"Diana..." he replied cautiously.
Their lips were almost touching as the need to actually kiss her and let his feelings run wild lingered in his head. He was aware of the dangers of developing this friendship with her colleague and acquaintance, but he didn't seem to notice. She was the only person that caused him to completely lose himself, and he was able to accept the consequences of his carelessness.
"If this is my retribution, then I'm a willing sucker for suffering," he thought, his words flying at him like missiles.
We're almost there...

Suddenly, a loud beep could be detected from the phone on which they were watching the movie. An incoming call from the Justice League really shattered their solemn moment.

Diana was about to walk out, disappointed.

As she was abruptly seized by The Dark Knight himself, she was beeping, dismissing the intrusion. He purposefully pulled Diana tight to him as he pressed his lips to hers.

Diana couldn't believe what was happening. She was sure he'd use the "saved by the whistle" justification to flee, but now he's right here, hugging her.

She didn't give a damn anymore. She didn't want someone to wake her up if this was a dream. Diana, inexperienced as she was, simply closed her eyes and welcomed Bruce's loving kiss. His hands caressing her lovely curves got her much more nervous for some reason. She could sense his tongue threatening to penetrate the very corners of her lips, which she gladly embraces.

Bruce's thoughts were now jumbled, particularly with the woman he'd been fantasizing about in his arms. He could sense chills tingling down his spine anytime she touched him, which made him more violent. His tongue was bouncing prone on the very edges of her mouth, playing a slow pace with Diana's tongue. He was in charge this time, so he had to be careful not to hurry, particularly because it was her first time. Bruce realized he ought to maintain a steady and moderate pace so she could comfortably keep up.

He breaks away from the embrace, their saliva like a thin string connecting to each other's mouth. Bruce looks at her, panting from the exercise they just completed. He found her eyes were filled with lust and affection, meaning she desired more. Bruce laughs to himself as he quietly whispers to her face, "I'm sorry it took so long." He could detect a faint gasp from her as he uttered the whisper.

"I now have you for myself, Bruce," she said quietly, "my and mine only."

Bruce responds with a chuckle, raising her head to gaze into her eyes. "You've always got me, princess," he says. He said it with sincerity.

Diana was delighted to hear him say those words because she knew he had always loved her. Diana has no reason now not to pounce on him and claim him for herself. So, with a wide grin on her face and her eyes fixed on his, she lunged at him to the bunk. The desire she was experiencing was too strong to put into words

. She offered him the same look that lionesses would offer their prey while stalking them down. She bent in near to sample his lips once more, fiercely assaulting the very corners of his mouth when her tongue met his. Diana's enthusiasm was too intense to bear, so the pace had shifted to swift and daring. The Amazon Princess was now in control of the romantic dance.

Diana eventually succumbed to her impulses when...

Another beep could be seen, this time from Bruce's tool belt. They came to a halt for a brief moment when Bruce cast a downward look.

She pulled off his tool belt and threw it on the other side without delay.

"No interruptions, My Dark Knight," she teased, her accent so seductive that Bruce shivered.

"No interruptions," he quietly muttered in answer, knowing full well that he had lost all power. When he kissed her hand, he grinned easily.

"I'm completely yours this evening."

And so their romantic dance began, their voices ringing to the very ends of the building, but fortunately, Bruce had a tool in his tool belt that he fitted, which is a sound-cancelling system that is unique to her room only, in case anything like this happened again in the future.

He had no doubt now as they continued their intimacy, becoming more and more passionate by the minute. This is her first time, and he's determined to make it the most memorable night she's ever had.